Nara Lake is an Australian housewife with a grown up family. Interests other than writing include historical research, especially that concerning pioneer days, gardening, conservation and fishing. Published work includes seven novels, and many short stories, articles, etc.

LOST WOMAN

In the nineteenth century, Clytie Furlong has fled to Australia from England — where she thought she might be accused of murdering her grandfather — and finds herself embroiled in the legend of a lost woman, shipwrecked and held amidst the swamps and forests of Gipp's Land by aborigines. Clytie becomes the easy prey of unscrupulous Quentin Lambert, who forces her to try and help him find his wife, lost in a shipwreck. There follows a nightmare journey across the wastelands of Australia before the grim truth is revealed . . .

Books by Nara Lake
Published by The House of Ulverscroft:

NARA LAKE

◆

LOST WOMAN

Complete and Unabridged

ULVERSCROFT
Leicester

First published in Great Britain

First Large Print Edition
published 2000

All characters and events in this novel,
except those of a definitely historical
nature, are fictitious.

British Library CIP Data

Lake, Nara
  Lost woman.—Large print ed.—
  Ulverscroft large print series: romance
  1. Love stories
  2. Large type books
  I. Title
  823.9'14 [F]

  ISBN 0–7089–4170–2

Published by
F. A. Thorpe (Publishing) Ltd.
Anstey, Leicestershire
Set by Words & Graphics Ltd.
Anstey, Leicestershire
Printed and bound in Great Britain by
T. J. International Ltd., Padstow, Cornwall

This book is printed on acid-free paper

1

They say that the country is, in spite of closer settlement and the gold rushes, largely as wild as it ever was. More ships have come to grief along that desolate coastline, where for nearly a hundred miles the surf pounds against a wide golden beach backed uniformly by high, scrub-covered dunes. Only two years since, according to a letter received from a friend, the blacks of the Lakes fought a battle against their old enemies from the mountains, and had to be sent on their respective ways by mounted policemen from Sale, which is the new name of the village once called Flooding Creek.

Most of the usable land is still held by the cattlemen under lease from the Crown, but the small farmers are moving in, and the blacks are almost totally dispossessed. The miners tramp or ride along that track from Port Albert, on their way to the goldfields in the high ranges where once the Lands Commissioner had found a ship's figurehead, which, he informed his superiors back in Melbourne, he was positive was the lost white woman of Gipps

Land. How often have I wondered about that? He was an honourable man, but was he perhaps thoroughly exasperated by the persistence of rumours that a white woman was held captive by the wild tribes, and the equal persistence of townspeople safely in Melbourne who insisted that this tragic prisoner must be found? Those who claim to know the ways of the nomad aboriginal people of Australia could think it unlikely that they would burden themselves on their wanderings with anything so cumbersome as a ship's figurehead.

Was there ever a white woman held amidst the wild swamps and forests of Gipps Land by black savages? Or was it a mad rumour, compounded out of boredom by isolated men on the flimsiest evidence? The story started when settlers at Port Albert found a piece of woman's clothing used to caulk a blackfellow's canoe. Then followed vague and probably misunderstood statements from local blacks about a rival tribe which kept a shipwrecked white woman prisoner. After this, the most trivial pieces of evidence were used to bolster up the story, including the discovery by whites of a drawing allegedly resembling a heart, scratched into boggy soil.

Twenty years ago, it was possible that a

white woman could have been held helpless in the wilderness of eastern Gipps Land, if she could have survived the brutality of a tribal woman's life. When the story finally reached Sydney and the same Governor Gipps after whom the province had been named, a check was made of those ships missing along that coastline. Few women travelled in small coastal vessels in those pioneer times, and before long, an interesting tale came to light — that of a barque, carrying settlers from the Scottish Highlands, which had been wrecked upon that surf-pounded coast not so long before. Amongst the missing was a woman, a hardy product of Scotland's storm-lashed isles, who could speak no English and was able to converse only in Gaelic.

Here was someone who could endure hardship, especially in a climate far milder than that of her native land, and was at the same time unable to communicate her plight through an English-speaking native.

This solution may have been influenced by the recent sufferings and rescue of Mrs Fraser, also a Scot, from Great Sandy Island, off the coast of what is now Queensland. Her ordeal at the hands of the cannibal blacks included seeing her husband murdered in cold blood, and undoubtedly this is why the far less well founded story from Gipps Land was given such credence.

No real proof has ever come to light, although, my informant says, the story still persists about the campfires of old stockmen who remember the first days of white settlement.

As I sit here by the window impatiently waiting for my broken ankle to mend, it is hard to realise that I was once part of that story. However, since that absurd accident when a stiff gust of wind caught under my crinoline as I was descending some steps, I have had plenty of time to go through my old notes and sketches. From time to time, I have been tempted to put my Gipps Land experiences down on paper, but our society would look askance at a respectable middle-aged lady who confessed to such mad indiscretions!

★ ★ ★

It all started, the Gipps Land part of it, anyway, on a cool August day in Sydney, New South Wales, in the year 1844. At the time, I was too humiliated to notice whether the temperature was below freezing or above the century, or whether it was raining or blowing that dusty, unpleasant wind they

4

called a 'brickfielder.'

There I was, imprisoned in a small office in a stone warehouse not far from the harbour, up a steep street leading from Sydney Cove, where they were still building the new quay. I stood there, full of defiance, trying to hide the shame I felt at being caught in this unfortunate imposture, and at the same time dreadfully angry at the rough way in which I had been hustled from my hiding place amidst the bales on the dock. My arms felt bruised from the manhandling I had received from the stevedores who had dragged me from the wharf where the brig *Kerry Lass* awaited her cargo.

The man behind the desk stared at me calmly, but with a sinking heart I thought I saw a certain flicker in those almost opaque light brown eyes.

'You can go,' he ordered my captors. 'I'll deal with this myself.'

The two men who had found me, and borne me, protesting at every step, to this lair, mumbled and turned to the door, whilst I tried again to escape by darting between them. It was no use. In a second I was pushed away, almost thrown back into the room, and the door closed in my face, by the ship owner, who had sprung forward from behind his desk.

5

'All right,' he said, after what seemed to be a very long pause, 'what have you to say for yourself?'

'I didn't mean any harm,' I replied, keeping my voice low and hoping that he had not realised the truth about me. 'I wanted to go to Melbourne, that's all.'

Purposely, I had tried to imitate the colonial twang, in the hope that the man would think me a native-born lad.

'By stowing away on my ship? Why did you want to go to Melbourne? It's a forsaken hole.'

'I've business there,' I muttered, speaking through my nose. 'I — I'm sorry, Mr Lambert, for the trouble I've caused.'

He uttered a disbelieving laugh, and then, taking me unawares, snatched off my cap, and grabbed my loose dungaree shirt, pulling it against my chest so that my sex was clearly identified. I turned scarlet with mortification. I was about to slap at that particular hand when he released the material.

'I thought so,' he said, in a very satisfied tone of voice. 'Now, young woman, what's your story? Your sweetheart has put you into the family way and you're chasing him down to Melbourne? Or have you been stealing your mistress's silver?'

'How dare you!' I retaliated, pulling myself

up very straight to my full five feet four inches, and sending him one of those cool and contemptuous glances, so typical of the Furlong family. I had inherited this aptitude from my father, along with my fair Furlong looks, and, I realise now, my regrettable impulsiveness.

'How *dare* you!' he snapped, obviously losing all patience. 'If you don't tell me the truth, young woman, I'll call the constable, and he'll get to the bottom of things quickly enough. Now, what is your name?'

I knew his, of course. It was Quentin Lambert, although there were those who preferred to nickname him Foxy. He was a ship owner, a merchant whose interests ranged the South Seas, and significantly in that old Sydney, he was an emancipist. Emancipist was the polite name given to a person who had been transported as a felon and had served his sentence, choosing to remain in the colony when he became a free man. In his own parlance, he had come out 'legally,' unlike the exclusives, who bragged about having come out 'free,' and were therefore known as 'illegitimates' by the coarser-mouthed members of New South Wales' very mixed society. My former employers were exclusive to the bootheels, and if they despised emancipists, they also

7

looked down their moderately well-bred noses at assisted passage migrants: like myself.

What really annoyed the exclusives was that some of the emancipists did so well for themselves. Mr Lambert, whose eyes glared at me from beneath his tawny brows, was one such example of a former felon doing very well for himself, although there were those who said that his propitious marriage to the daughter of an already established merchant had helped.

'My name,' I stated haughtily, after a moment's thought, 'is Smith.'

I had become quite determined over the past minutes that no former transportee, sent out to New South Wales for heaven only knew what evil crimes, was going to browbeat me.

'Smith?'

Mr Lambert looked down at his coat, and flicked at a speck of fluff which had settled on the dark blue material. Unlike many of Sydney's upstarts, who tended to retain their rough mode of speech and dress while their womenfolk paraded in silks, he was something of a dandy, and barbered with style and care.

When he spoke again, it was in a ruminating, half-mocking way which put me more than ever on my guard.

'Smith? Er — from the English branch or the Irish division of the family?'

'I'm English,' I said, and wished that I had been more original.

'And your first name, Miss Smith?'

Because I was angry, I answered too quickly, and then could have kicked myself. Oh why, why, had I not said Emma, or Harriet, or Maria?

'Clytie.'

'Clytie?' Mr Lambert looked puzzled, and for a moment I felt triumphant. For all his fine clothes, superior accent and air of being utterly in control of every situation, this emancipist captor of mine must surely lack that knowledge of the classics necessary to every gentleman.

'Clytie?' he repeated, as if to himself. 'Clytie Smith. I dare say it's possible.'

'Clytie,' I said patiently, 'was a nymph in Greek mythology.'

'I'm quite aware of that. The foolish girl fell in love with Apollo, pined away, and was turned into a flower. *Not* a sunflower, as some say. The sunflower as we knew it wasn't discovered by Europeans until the conquest of Peru.'

Then, abruptly, he lost interest in botany and history, and looked me up and down with such calculation that I had a presentiment that whatever Mr Lambert had in store for me, it was not pleasant.

'I want the whole story,' he demanded, harshly. 'The whole story. The truth about yourself.'

2

The whole story, the truth. Where did I start? Oh yes, I could have given him the whole story, but I doubted whether he had the patience or the time to hear it through.

The truth was that the story of my misfortunes started with my birth.

I preferred to call myself Furlong, but Starling would have done as well. I had lived with my father until nigh unto my seventeenth year, but he had never done anything to make my position regular, and to call me Furlong was to give me that to which I was not entitled. My mother, who had died a few months after my birth, was born Susan Starling, and left this world the same way.

Poor Susan had been a housemaid in my father's establishment, and apparently had been both prettier and warmer than his legal wife. When necessity had forced his flight to Italy after I was born, he took us both with him, but my mother was unhappy in a foreign country, and my father always maintained that she had died as much from homesickness as from fever. My father was

11

not a man to bury his heart, and soon found consolation with a series of mistresses. It must have been a relief to his family to have him safely out of Britain. They could have overlooked his roving eye, but he was also possessed of a burning sense of injustice and not much stability of character.

His branch of the Furlongs had sprung from an impoverished young Scot who had joined the East India Company, and, having survived many dangers, had returned to settle in England with malaria and great wealth. He made a good marriage, bought a large country estate, but lived barely long enough to see his son reach his first birthday. This child became my paternal grandfather, but before he attained his majority, coal was discovered on his land. It was the time of change. The small village which had been the centre of life there since the Middle Ages now had the two vitals of industry, coal and water. Together, they made steam, and steam powered the mills.

Gaunt brick buildings with ever-smoking chimneystacks grew where before there had been pleasant pasturage. About them, mean little rows of houses proliferated to become warrens for the new breed of Englishman, the mill worker, the wage slave trapped into a system as cruel as that which held his black brethren captive. My grandfather, from being a fairly rich landowner, now became very wealthy indeed, and a good marriage paved the way for the next generation to move another step upwards towards the aristocracy.

My father, second surviving son of Frederick Furlong, was early marked out for a brilliant career. He was clever and had a charming manner, and after his elder brother was killed in Spain, all my widowed grandfather's hopes must have centred upon him. What a disappointment my father turned out to be. He had no interest in the gentlemen's clubs for which he was nominated by his mother's influential family. Long before Lord Shaftsbury made it fashionable, he took up the cause of the poor workers who had been taken from their slummy cottage industries and pushed by economic pressures into the more efficient but inhuman mills. He decided to set England to rights, not by being elected to the House of Commons as his ambitious family intended, but by far more drastic means.

His radical activities culminated, after many stormy family quarrels, at the debacle on St Peter's Field at Manchester, better known as Peterloo. This vast assemblage of sixty thousand had no design but peaceful protest against the system which kept their lives under the control of a tiny privileged group. The men, women and children who streamed in orderly fashion to St Peter's Field came unprepared for violence. My father was there amongst them, handing out his pamphlets (printed with Furlong money), demanding universal franchise, an annual parliament, and the other items which made up the radical cause.

What happened at Peterloo is common knowledge. After Mr Hunt, a well-known radical orator, had arrived to address the multitude, the authorities, belatedly, decided to arrest him. Yeomanry were sent in to support constables assigned to this task, and with remarkable stupidity, charged into the peaceful crowd, which, put to the test, stood fast. Thus it came about that the Yeomanry, the amateur troops, were caught in that great throng of people. The 15th Hussars, standing by in case of an emergency, were then sent in to rescue the Yeomanry, and within a few minutes most of the people who had come peacefully to St Peter's Fields were in flight, leaving behind several dead and hundreds of injured. My father lay on the fields of Peterloo, in agony from a broken leg. He had tripped over a pole, bearing a placard, which had been dropped by a fleeing workman.

This experience, and his narrow escape from a prison sentence, chastened him for a while. It must have been during the time that he was held captive, as it were, by his broken leg, that he was persuaded into marriage with a 'suitable' young woman.

It was a failure. My father was a passionate man in every sense. Whether it was a cause or a woman, he had to embrace it hotly, and he and his wife soon discovered that they had almost nothing in common. They produced two sons to ensure continuation of the Furlong name, and my father began his association with my mother. His radical friends were as annoyed as the Furlong family. To them, loose living was the hallmark of the Old Order. Radicals were respectable.

The ultimate disaster arrived soon after my birth. There came to light some extremely foolish letters father had written, a few years previously, to one Arthur Thistlewood, instigator of the infamous Cato Street Conspiracy back in 1820. Thistlewood's plot to murder the entire Cabinet as they dined together was exposed in time, and he and four of his accomplices were executed. Father's promise of aid to this violent and silly scheme ruined his reputation on every side, and he retreated to Italy. He had a

15

modest income left to him by a maternal uncle who had died before realising that William Furlong was a black sheep, and we lived quite comfortably in a small villa on the outskirts of Naples.

Here, I grew up carefree and untrammelled, watched over casually by a series of Italian servants, and tutored by my clever father into the mysteries of English grammar, history, geography and, naturally, social philosophy. I much preferred my drawing pad to my text books, but most of my impractical education stuck. Of course, I did not have my father's undivided attention. I had to share that with his writing and with a succession of mistresses of almost every European nationality.

Some I liked. Some I loathed; but before my twelfth birthday, I had discovered that whatever my feelings towards them, they were never a permanent feature of life at the villa. In between these episodes with their wild, passionate beginnings, their quarrels, and their inevitable fading, I received additions to my education. Whilst girls at home were stitching samplers, poor things, I was wandering about unmatched Capri, or visiting eerie Pomeii. There was once a holiday in stately Rome, and for six months, when cholera struck Naples, we lived in Florence.

My childhood then, was unsettled, pagan, and in many ways guaranteed to make the righteous-minded throw up their hands in horror, but, looking back, I can recall many sunny, laughing days, and in my memory I hear still the songs of the peasants at harvest time and sniff the rich odour of grapes ready for the press. Sometimes, there were warm afternoons and wine-touched evenings, when I sat unnoticed in a corner, listening to the arguments and clever talk of visiting exiles who, like my father, had taken up residence in Italy because of scandal and shortage of funds.

When I was fifteen, my father did start again giving serious thought to my future; but when he met Antoinette he pushed the matter aside for the time being. Each year since I had turned twelve, he mentioned the quite important question of what life held in store for me, and each year, his attention strayed to a new love.

I do not know where he met Antoinette, but then, I was never very sure how he met any of those fleeting attachments. One day, the small villa with the glorious glimpses of Naples' incomparable Bay betwixt the cypresses would be ours alone, if one excepted the servants. The next, I would be an outsider, making do with the companionship of the village children and the servants. But now, I was nearly sixteen, and past the age of village children. My Neapolitan contemporaries had grown, too, and the boys with whom I had played ball or hide and seek were lusty youths, forward and eager for conquest in the Italian way. So, Antoinette's arrival heralded a lonely time for me.

The Furlongs at the villa received no formal acceptance from the consular set. Father would occasionally be invited to men's evening parties with his fellow expatriates, because of his wit and good connections back home, but British women of standing could not be expected to put themselves out for his wild, skinny, out-of-wedlock daughter.

Amongst our little retinue of servants, old Paolo, our porter and general handyman, Maria, his wife and our cook, and Serafina, who did everything they would not touch, it was with the last that I enjoyed friendship of a kind. Serafina came from a remote village where the inhabitants had not quite made up their minds to whom they owed their souls, the Church or the Devil. She was tall for a southern Italian, a rangy, hawk-featured girl with bold black eyes and a nature both kindly and gullible. She shared my feelings about Antoinette, and expressed her opinion of the newcomer in a Calabrian term which

18

I prefer not to remember.

Antoinette was the best looking of the women who had paraded through my father's rakish life. She was, I think, nudging thirty, although her fair skin was unlined and her figure trim. She seemed to have some of that gloss known as breeding, and why she should have chosen to live with my father, who was then in his forty-fifth year, and showing signs of a constitution weakened by consumption and dissipation, remains a mystery to this day. Such are the ways of love.

She was French, as should be apparent by her name, donated, no doubt, by royalist sympathiser parents for the vain and foolish queen who died beneath the guillotine. She was also, when not entrancing my father with her vivacity, jealous and possessed of what can only be described as 'French-ness.' That is, she had the maddening Gallic conviction that the mere fact of being French excused her every fault and set her above women of every other race. I hated her. She enjoyed pointing out that someone as awkward and plain as myself was not likely to have male admirers, let alone a husband.

Now, I knew that I was too thin, and that my face was a little too angular and my eyes too baby blue and big; but my father said that I lived up to my nymph's name, with

19

my fair hair and fey looks, and I was not unaware that certain men who visited the villa were beginning to make a fuss of me. When this last happened, so that Antoinette was briefly not the centre of attention, she went out of her way to cut me down with a deft remark. She was jealous of my still unspoiled youthfulness, but always managed to make me appear to be the one at fault.

As I prayed for Antoinette's hasty exit from my father's life, Serafina was undergoing worries of her own. Serafina was in love, and longed to marry, but the courtship had dragged on for three years.

The trouble was that Pasquale hailed from Sicily. I liked Pasquale, who was a plumpish, jolly man in his thirties, with surprisingly pale skin and light eyes for one from a Mediterranean country. He was a seafaring man, the mate on a small ship plying the Italian seaboard and, despite all the stories one hears about sailors, I think that he really meant to marry Serafina. But, as I have mentioned, he was from Sicily, and on that island they have a custom which makes it a little hard for a man to marry when the fancy takes him. The sons of a family are expected to remain single until their sisters are safely wed or settled in a convent, and Serafina's sailor had three sisters who were particular about their suitors. So, the years slipped by, and one sister married, while the other two remained at home, making lace and embroidering and passing their days in the security provided by their parents and three bachelor brothers. The custom, I believe, went back to the times when Saracen raiders descended without warning upon Italian seaport towns, snatching girls for the slave market. For the preservation of the race, it was necessary for every Christian girl to have several young males at hand to protect her.

Serafina had reached a state of desperation, for she was twenty-five and without a dowry, and Pasquale was the only man interested in her. She told me that she was going to see a woman from her own home village who now lived in Naples, dispensing charms and telling fortunes. She was nervous about going alone, and anyway, where is the young girl who does not wish to know what the future holds for her? We went one afternoon, in what passed for autumn in that southern climate, when the leaves fell yellow from the vines and the olive trees stood sad and dark under the greying skies.

3

The fortune teller lived in a filthy room at the end of a stinking alley. The place terrified me, and I drew the black shawl Serafina had lent me closer across my fair hair as lounging men lurking in doorways made suggestive remarks in the coarsest of gutter Neapolitan. At last, we reached the seer's hovel, and after an exchange between Serafina and an invisible person inside, the occupant revealed herself and beckoned us to enter. We sat ourselves on stools, and after some further talk in a mountain patois which I could not follow, a coin changed hands, and Serafina held out her palm for the old witch's inspection.

She was a hideous old woman, almost toothless, with a seamed and sallow skin and a marked moustache. Ragged black garments were clutched about her, emitting a suffocating odour compounded of stale perspiration and garlic every time she moved, and I wanted nothing more than to run from this evil hole. Whatever it was that she told Serafina pleased my companion, and then those black buttons of eyes, set in a web of wrinkles, fixed on myself. She shot several words at Serafina, who answered in the same dialect, and turning to me, our servant asked whether I wanted my fortune told.

I needed little persuading. I found a coin, and extended my palm. The crone took it, stared down, and then thrust it away, spitting out sentences at Serafina, who crossed herself and looked quite stricken.

'What is it?' I asked Serafina, and the poor young woman looked away from me.

Now that horrible old creature was eager to be rid of us, and in contrast, the air in the alley seemed quite pure as we were hurried out of the room.

'You must tell me,' I insisted, as we scuttled down a steep and broken flight of steps leading to a more salubrious thoroughfare.

'No, I cannot. Forget it. It'll only make you sad.'

'Tell me!' There must have been something intimidating in my voice, because she stopped and looked at me, her fine eyes clouded and wary.

'She doesn't like foreigners. Perhaps that's why she said — she said that you were a lost soul.' Serafina took a deep breath and crossed herself yet again. 'Wherever you turn, there will be death.'

In the middle of the sheltered square into which we merged from the maze of slum alleyways, the late afternoon sun now smiled warm and mellow despite the passing of summer. But I felt a cold chill steal through me, and, being the child of a free thinking lapsed Protestant and without the benefit of religious education, I could not even resort to Serafina's protective crossing of herself.

What did that evil witch mean by a lost soul? That I was going to die soon, that I had the Evil Eye, a very real affliction in southern Italy, or that I was doomed to live in the manner of my father's many mistresses, exchanging lovers as other women changed their dresses, or simply, that I did not belong to the True Faith?

'Wherever you turn, there will be death.'

If it had been meant to scare me, it succeeded. I crept home in Serafina's wake, frightened and subdued. Was it possible that the crone had known that I had wished — no, prayed — that my tormentor, Antoinette, would die?

Yet, as October's days slid away, I began to forget this experience. My father talked again of my future, and egged on by hateful Antoinette, who was usually preening and pouting in the near background during out discussions, now dropped his bombshell. I

24

was to return to England!

Return to England! I could hardly believe my ears, for I had been carried from my native land in my mother's arms. The exiles hereabouts talked often of English things and the new Queen and the good times they had had before circumstances had driven them to this alien shore, but they might as well have been talking about the moon as far as I was concerned. I had read father's English books eagerly enough, but the wild border men of Scott's novels and the stiff-mannered ladies and gentlemen created by Jane Austen were no more real to me than the odd persons who prowled through the Gothic stories I preferred. Real people spoke Italian southern-style in raucous, happy voices, and arranged their years about the dictates of a Church which took so many of them into its cloisters. This was the land of harsh sun, olive groves, pasta, and of ancient ruins which were so much a part of daily life that they hardly seemed like ruins at all.

Vesuvius, not the White Cliffs of Dover, was the landmark of my life. My father had told me about England's great industries, but I could not even begin to imagine a country scarred and blackened, where so many spent their working days in steamy mills, and where the skies were perpetually stained by smoke. Much of Neapolitan life was squalid and poverty-stricken, but there was always the hot summer sun and the blue, blue Tyrrhenian Sea.

'But what would I do there?' I faltered.

My father smiled at me as he sipped his wine, and yet, later I recalled that his eyes were wary, and sad.

'It would be best in the long run,' he said. 'I hope to arrange to apprentice you to a milliner — one of the good society milliners where you would learn the best of the trade and make good contacts and perhaps be able to set up for yourself in time. I've an elderly cousin living in London with whom I've been corresponding. She'll be happy to provide you with a home. Eventually, I trust, my little nymph, you'll meet a decent young man and marry. But until then, some provision must be made for your future and your well-being.'

A milliner! I could speak, read and write Italian, sketch well, hold my own in a conversation about the classics, write a good hand in English — and could hardly thread a needle. For the first time I realised the great gulf between male and female life, and I hated it intensely.

'She's made you decide this!' I cried, sending a passionate glance towards Antoinette, who, unable to understand more than a few words of English, shrugged and stared back in that assured way of hers.

'Clytie! That isn't so.' My father turned to his mistress and spoke to her sharply in French, and she left the room, flouncing a little as she walked away.

'Now, listen to me,' he said, with unusual sternness. 'I don't want you to go, Clytie. You're all the family I have now. But you're old enough now to understand your position. My health isn't what it was, child, and the last thing I want is for you to be left alone here in a foreign country.'

'It isn't foreign. It's my home.' I retorted, trying to hold back my tears. 'And if you are ill, you need me.'

'You're going back to England,' he stated, in a voice which allowed for no argument. 'Clytie, you know that you have two half-brothers, my sons. The income which has supported us here goes to them when I die. There will be nothing for you, except some small royalties from my books.'

For the first time in my short life I understood fully the ignominy of my position. I was only Clytie Starling. If I had really been Clytie Furlong, I would have been sent to a young ladies' seminary back home, to be brushed and polished up for an entry into correct society. Honour demanded that my father make some arrangements for my future, but according to custom, it needed only to be a second class future.

'Oh, my dear child!' He put down his wine glass and reached for my hand. 'I wouldn't have it so. My sons already have their future assured, but unfortunately, the capital which provides my income is entailed. When I die, it has to pass on to Tom, your elder half-brother.'

Miserable though I was, I saw the sadness in his eyes, and understood, again for the first time, how he must have missed his sons all these years.

'I wrote to Tom and Horace last week,' he then told me. 'I've asked them to take an interest in you. I don't know whether they will find it in their hearts to do it, but . . .'

With a sigh, he arose, and walked across the paved floor to the window overlooking the vineyards which stretched away on the landward side of our house.

'Your life is stretching out in front of you, just like the view out there. Do your best with it, Clytie.'

'Are you very ill?' I asked, timidly, and then, with horrible clarity, the fortune teller's words came back to me. Had she meant that my father was going to die?

'Not very, Clytie. But I have to accept that I won't make old bones. Now that we've discussed it, I'll see the British consul as soon as I can and arrange a safe passage for you back to England.'

'I can't go. I can't leave you!' I said stubbornly, but I knew it was no use. My father had made up his mind.

Dinner that night was a subdued meal, and a little earlier than usual, because our servants wished to go to Mass, it being All Hallows' Eve. Antoinette was Catholic, too, but to partake of the Host meant that she would have to make her confession, and I think she was wary of that. It was a dinner I would never forget, although at the time, I was so wretched that I wanted it over quickly so that I could escape to the relief of tears in my own room. My father and Antoinette spoke and joked and laughed in their curious mixture of Italian and French, and Antoinette, who by this time knew that my fate had been decided, looked very confident and pleased with herself.

A Frenchwoman, her manner seemed to say, knew instinctively how to manage a man, and she had handled my father very much to her own satisfaction. Not for the first time, I wondered how it was that Antoinette, who knew so much about men, had not found herself a rich and aristocratic husband, or, at least, a protector better endowed with wealth than my father.

So, I went up to bed, and indulged in a fit of sulky fancies. I would run away, and become the mistress of one of those Italian princes who lived in medieval grandeur on great estates. Perhaps I would go to the British consulate and throw myself on the mercy of a handsome young official who would immediately fall madly in love with me and marry me. Or, I would persuade Serafina to smuggle me to her village, and we would pretend that I had been kidnapped by brigands, and my father would be so remorseful that he would completely change his mind about sending me to England. I was one mass of silly schemes, all overlaid by my hatred of Antoinette, who, I was more convinced than ever, had persuaded my father to be rid of me.

At some time during the evening, I fell asleep as I lay sprawled across my bed, and when I awoke, the house was very quiet, and I was very cold, for I was uncovered, and clad only in my nightgown.

Somewhere, in the distance, a bell tolled mournfully, and it was with a start that I realised that it was midnight. The villa was still and dark, except for my own candle, which I now snuffed. The servants had long ago returned, and all was safely locked up against the dangers of the outside world. Then, as I was about to climb between the sheets, I paused. There was someone at the gate, and I could hear old Paolo complaining that it was too late to wake the master.

'There is no need for that,' replied a strange voice in execrable Italian. 'I shall do it myself.'

Surprised, I ran across to the window which overlooked our small walled garden at the front of the villa. My room was only on the first floor, but the ground sloped sufficiently so that I could see over the wall out on to the roadway, and there, shadowy in the dim light of a crescent moon which hung between the scudding clouds on this most ghostly of all nights, stood a large and saddled horse of dark colour. In another instant, I saw its owner, or rather, the silhouette of a tall, very thin person, wrapped in a long cloak and wearing a broad-brimmed hat of the kind preferred by brigands, or French curés, or, as I learnt much later, by frontiersmen. Even in full light, this hat would have obscured the features of the visitor, who, having pushed poor Paolo aside as he attempted to stop this intrusion, passed out of my sight under our portico.

I heard the footsteps bound up the stairs as Paolo ranted and shouted, and fear clutched at me. Who was this? Only the harbinger of evil tidings would act thus, and at such an hour. Was he a fiend unleashed during this night of the dead? (In those days, I was too strongly impressed by the weird tales invented by Gothic novelists.)

'Who's there? What's all the commotion?' It was my father's voice, angry and in English. Then: 'Who the hell are you?'

There was no reply. That was the most macabre feature of the ghastly events about to take place. Like a mute, or the fiend I had imagined him to be, the visitor said not a word, and excepting that I had already heard him speak, outside, in very bad Italian, I should have imagined for the rest of my days that he was quite bereft of the power of human speech.

'No! No!'

What had happened? Why had my father cried out in that strange way, his voice trailing off into a gurgle? Why was Antoinette screaming now, as if confronted by all the devils in the pit?

'Tu! Non, Mon Dieu, non!'

Her scream pierced through the very tiles

of the villa's roof, and I heard the clatter of riding boots down the stairs, and old Paolo shouting, and our female servants yelling, while I, pitiful little coward that I was, hid in my room, momentarily paralysed by a fear so deep that I was as if frozen. Then, somehow, I found the courage to open the door, and Serafina was there, holding a candle, her swarthy peasant's face whiter than the cap on her black hair. She was praying rapidly, crossing herself, and no doubt asking God's mercy for the souls which had fled the two poor bodies which lay lifeless on the tiled floor, their blood oozing to the very top of the stairs, where it began an unspeakable trickle downwards.

Serafina turned and saw me, half fainting in my doorway, and with some presence of mind, she forgot her own terror, and pushed me back into the bedroom, slamming the door behind me. I had seen them, though, my father bleeding from an enormous wound in his chest, and Antoinette with her pretty, silly head almost severed from her body.

They said that a sabre, covered in blood from hilt to point, which was found discarded on the roadway outside, was the instrument used, and poor old Paolo had to explain that this fearful weapon had been hidden by the murderer's long cloak. No, he had never seen the man before, and knew nothing about him except that he was a foreigner judging by the way he mistreated the language. The sabre was of a type used by Napoleon's dragoons during the long wars which had ended a quarter of a century before.

The man who slaughtered my father and his mistress was never brought to justice. Who was he, husband, lover, father, brother? That he was part of Antoinette's past I did not doubt. My father had been despatched with one clean thrust to the heart. For Antoinette there had been a swinging blow meant to decapitate her.

And for me, there was a burden of guilt. I had wished her dead so many times, and the hideous old fortune teller in that slum hovel had told me that I was a lost soul. Was I afflicted with an evil power?

Grief for my father was deep, but eased in time. The added feeling that I was in some way responsible was a load I was to carry for many years.

4

Strangely, I wept very little, and was still in my state of dazed shock when one of my father's English friends took me to see the British consul. I would have to go home, they said, and this time there was no argument in me. I was listless with sorrow and guilt, and wanted nothing but to escape forever from the dreadful events at our pretty villa with its matchless glimpses of the blue, blue Tyrrhenian Sea.

As I passed for the first time through the cool marble entrance hall of the consul's residence, I could not help remembering that Lord Nelson must have walked here many times, long ago, when ladies of fashion, like Emma Hamilton, wore light, flowing muslins and had their hair cut into short, almost boyish curls. Poor Lord Nelson. Poor Emma.

The consul was sympathetic but matter of fact. The problems of persons who found themselves in distress far from solid, safe Britain were commonplace to him, and he lost no time in solving mine. An English couple with young children were travelling to London shortly, and as they did not wish to take their Italian nurse with them, I could go with them in that capacity. This fixed, he now came to what was the nub of the matter.

'Miss Starling,' he began.

'Furlong,' I corrected him, and he appeared a little taken aback.

To cover this awkwardness, he sent for a glass of ratafia for my comfort. Then, he continued.

'Documents taken from your father's papers had given me the impression that Starling is your legal name,' he told me.

'I was his daughter. I am Clytie Amanda Furlong,' I replied, refusing to be budged on this, and he let it go.

'Now,' he said, very kindly, 'your father's will and so on are being sent to England, and in due course his estate will be probated. Miss — Miss Furlong, I must tell you this. There is nothing for you.'

'I know that, sir,' I replied, forcing the words to come past the choking in my throat.

He seemed greatly relieved that there were not going to be hysterics and vapours.

'I don't doubt that he meant to make provision for you during his lifetime, and in fact, Miss Furlong, he recommended in his will that your half-brothers should take care of you in the event of his own early death.'

'What if they don't want me?'

Where had all those happy days of my childhood gone?

A servant came in with the glass of ratafia on a small silver salver, and the consul took it and courteously handed it to me. I drank it, too upset to taste it. Then he looked down at me from his splendid height, the gravity in his eyes belying the smile on his lips.

'I'm sure that they will do their duty.'

Their duty! How cold and uncertain that sounded. I thought again about poor Emma Hamilton, who had once lived in this handsome villa. England had painted her as a scarlet woman, ignored its hero's wishes, and cast her aside. When people are dead, I brooded, morbidly, they can't make others do what they want any more, not unless it is arranged in such a way that they *have* to.

★ ★ ★

I arrived in London a few days after Christmas, and was left, trembling with nervousness, at the home of Mrs Sophie Birrell, that widowed cousin of my father's with whom it was intended that I should live when I became apprenticed. She lived very quietly in a semi-fashionable area inhabited mostly by persons like herself, of gentle upbringing and connections, and somewhat modest means. Some prosperous tradespeople were beginning to move into the district, and their wives' more ostentatious ways and pushing attempts to improve their social standing were already causing some consternation amidst their conservative neighbours.

Still, in spite of what the old ladies in Mrs Birrell's circle considered a positive upheaval in the settled order of things, life there was extremely quiet and dull. I did not mind this. It gave me time to mend a little, and recover somewhat from that dreadful memory of the night when my father and Antoinette had been so brutally murdered.

Mrs Birrell had been my paternal grandmother's best friend as a girl, and eventually, my father's godmother. Throughout all his vicissitudes, she had retained an affection for him, and although she passed me off as a distant relative rather than explain my true standing to her friends, she was kindness itself. However, I soon realised that the consul at Naples, when he had written to her about my father's death and my consequent journey to England, had glossed over the circumstances of that fatal All Hallows' Eve. She, poor innocent lady, thought that he had been killed by a burglar, and I had the sense to hold my tongue.

I heard nothing from the Furlongs, although I knew that they had been notified of the tragedy, and when I confided to Mrs Birrell that my brothers had been asked to take care of me, she pursed her lips and glanced at me with a sudden and uncharacteristic worldliness in her round blue eyes.

'I wouldn't set much store by that, child. Your position *is* irregular, and you must realise that your brothers are still under age. Tom reaches his majority this year, and Horace is a year younger.'

This should have been obvious to me all along, for all the boys had been still in skirts when our father had run away with my mother.

'I dare say that Will assumed that some years would elapse before Tom and Horace were put to the test. Have you considered becoming a governess, my dear?'

This question followed on the other remarks so quickly that I knew it to be her way of telling me not to put any hope at all on the Furlongs. Yet, the very next day, upon returning from taking Mrs Birrell's small and spoilt dog for a walk, I was informed by Clara, the maidservant, that a Mr Parker awaited me in the drawing-room.

I knew of no Mr Parker, but nevertheless hastened to the drawing-room, conscious of being a little windblown after my walk. There Mrs Birrell, who had the look of a woman who had been making strained conversation, immediately introduced me to the stout man in his thirties, who had been warming his coat tails before the fire, and keeping most of the warmth from the rest of the room on this chilly afternoon. This was my cousin, Franklin Parker, the son of my father's only sister, and he had come to escort me to Furlong Hall!

My dislike for the newcomer was instant. He had a look about him which was at once mean and self-indulgent, a hint of having been the sort of child who stuffed himself with sweets in a corner rather than share with others.

'How do you do, cousin?' he said, advancing to take my hand, which I withdrew as quickly as I could, for he somehow managed to combine a meaning caress with the handshake.

'It appears that your father's family wishes to meet you,' explained Mrs Birrell, in the hushed voice of one who is utterly surprised. From the way in which she spoke, I understood that I was to have no say in the affair. It had all been arranged.

'Do try,' said Mrs Birrell, later, as she supervised my small amount of packing, 'to please your grandfather, my dear. You cannot hope to have your position made more *regular*, but, my dear, a small allowance would make such a difference! You could stay here with me instead of having to wrack your brains trying to think of some way of earning a living. A milliner! Whatever put such an idea into Will's head?'

I knew that it was not 'what,' but Antoinette who had put that idea into my father's head, but I said meekly that my father had thought that it would be best for me. At the same time, I was aware that Mrs Birrell's circumstances were straitened, and that my presence here had meant a further strain upon her small domestic resources.

'Oh, my dear,' she burst out then, dabbing at her eyes, 'I'll pray that everything goes well with you. Frederick — your grandfather — has always been a difficult and haughty man, but perhaps old age has mellowed him a little.' She smiled, and touched my cheek. 'If anyone can reach his heart, it is you, my dear. You are the image of your

41

grandmother. I think that is why I liked you immediately.'

Looking back, it is hard to describe how I felt as I set forth on my fresh journey. I was frightened, a little puzzled and, perhaps, a shade hopeful. Yet, at the same time, I had a strange sensation of being borne along, as if I had no will, and were being directed by a force outside myself. Within the dull security of Mrs Birrell's house, I had almost, briefly, escaped the torments which had descended upon me on that evil day when I had visited the witch's hovel.

I arrived at the Furlong's fine mansion on a melancholy day in early spring, when, although some blossom had been opening further south, the wind howled through still leafless trees, and a solitary bird endeavouring to pull a worm from the dormant lawn looked as huddled and miserable as the unemployed mill workers I had seen in the towns through which we had passed. Nevertheless, it was a relief to reach our destination. For one thing, the weather had been foul, and I was thoroughly homesick for Italy's milder climate. For another, Franklin's behaviour had confirmed all my forebodings. He considered that a young female relative born into a precarious state in life was fair prey, and when I made my feelings clear, he became extremely unpleasant.

If he had had his way, he said, my existence would have been completely ignored. Well, as far as he was concerned, I was just that fool Will's bastard, and I needn't come to him expecting his help.

'My father was your uncle,' I answered, stiff with misery and anger. 'You should show more respect.'

'Respect!' sneered Franklin, as the carriage proceeded along a drive through the landscaped gardens near the house, and I, eager to see my destination, ignored him as I peered out of the carriage window.

This was not the house where my father had spent his boyhood. That older dwelling, it had been decided a decade earlier, was too near the town which had added to the Furlong's wealth, and too small and inconvenient besides. This one, erected on a remoter part of the estate, was in a fine mock Tudor style, designed in a fashion which would have been as foreign to Good Queen Bess as the evilly smoking stacks smudging the horizon beyond the parks and woods.

I was handed from the carriage on to a finely raked gravelled forecourt, and, beyond the terrace, a heavy oaken front door opened, held thus by a tall man in a stiff livery. I guessed that he was a footman, for I was already beginning to distinguish well-trained British staff from the sloppy, goodnatured lot who had passed for servants in my father's villa. No mysterious midnight visitor could have bluffed his way into this mansion.

Franklin strode past me into the house, my little bit of luggage was whisked off somewhere, and I was left to cool my heels — and I mean this literally, as the tiny flicker in the grate warmed no more than a few square inches right by the hearth — in a sort of ante room. I wanted to weep.

Eventually, there was a summons, and I was led into a vast, book-lined room, where a cruel-mouthed old man stood before a fire, leaning on a cane. This elderly person, I knew without being told, was my paternal grandfather, but there was no welcome or family recognition. He regarded me without favour for some moments, taking in my Italian-styled black clothes, which were in too light a fabric for this climate, and in time his gimlet eyes alighted upon the silver cross which hung from a chain about my neck. It had been given to me as a parting gift by the servants at the villa, not so much, I think, as a religious symbol, but as a memento.

'You're Catholic?' he snarled at me.

'No,' I answered.

'Well, I suppose one has to be thankful for something.'

That was my welcome to Furlong Hall.

My luggage had been taken up to what was to be my room, and as I followed a sour-faced maid upstairs, I began to wonder very seriously just why I had been summoned to Furlong Hall. My arrival seemed to be a matter of annoyance rather than of joy, and my quarters indicated my position very nicely. A proper guest room would have signified acceptance. Therefore, I was given a cramped little closet of a room which had been designed to shelter a governess. It had a tiny window which overlooked a narrow and depressing courtyard, meant, I think, more as a light well than as a place of outdoor use.

The whole exercise of bringing me to them, I reasoned, as I wearily unloosened the strings of my bonnet and slipped off my cloak, was to convince the world that they had done their duty. No servant came to help me unpack: this would have been too kind. I stowed away my possessions as best I could, and set out my toilet things. The face looking back at me from the mirror as I tidied my hair was pinched, tired, and too young to hide the resentment boiling up inside me.

There was a small stack of books on the

night table, meant, no doubt, to console me in my time of grief. I picked up the top one. The title was, 'Morals from the Graveyard.'

After what seemed a very long time, a bell summoned me to dinner downstairs, and now I had the opportunity to study my relatives. There was Grandfather, Franklin, a pair of spinster ladies who were the issue of my father's elder brother who had died fighting Napoleon, and, of course, my father's widow, a gaunt woman who stared at me with a glacial hatred. In time, I was to learn that my cousin Franklin, who was the son of my father's also-deceased sister (the Furlongs of that generation were not given to longevity), had a wife. She, being able to please herself by reason of a well-tied-up fortune, had long since retreated to the brighter attractions of the South. Of my half-brothers, into whose care my father had so optimistically placed me, there was no sign.

A fortnight dragged past, dull and lonely to a degree, and nothing was said about plans for my future. From the servants, and one or two conversations with my spinster cousins, who seemed to spend their lives in twittering nervousness, I did find out a little about the occupants of Furlong Hall. My cousin Franklin was virtually manager of the family businesses and estates, although it was intended that my brothers, who were still at university, would take over some of the responsibility in due course. I also learnt that my grandfather, after a lifetime spent in the pursuit of wealth, was in failing health, despite his erect stance and fierce manner.

It seemed to be the rule of the house that one made one's own way except at mealtimes. Mrs Furlong, who had never once spoken a word to me, received callers and made calls, although there were times when she was confined to her room by some unspecified malady. The two furtive spinsters apparently filled in their useless days going for pleasing walks when the weather allowed, and working at endless embroideries. They were, I thought, scared of me, and in the wretched night hours I thought often of that dreadful fortune teller. Had she been right? Was there about me an aura which warned others to keep their distance? Was I afflicted with the Evil Eye?

The real explanation did not occur to me. To those painfully shy and timid women, I must have seemed unbelievably gauche and badly brought up, coming as I did from the kind of background which is today fashionable to call Bohemian.

I badly wanted to ask whether I could

be sent back to Mrs Birrell, but the opportunity did not come. At this time, both my cousin Franklin and my grandfather were absorbed in a campaign against the stopping of transportation to the Australian colonies. There was Furlong money invested in sheep raising there, and a supply of cheap labour was necessary to keep up the profits, convicts having been employed for this purpose. However, public feeling both here in Britain and in New South Wales had turned against the convict system, and a bill had just been approved at Westminster for the discontinuation of the practice. Having been reared in a foreign country, I knew very little about the cause of my relatives' anger, and it was by reading some handbills which Franklin had had printed that I learned something of the issue. It meant little to me then, for all I was interested in was the chance of escaping from this gloomy mansion.

5

Later, I would be told by my fiancé that raising sheep in vast numbers on unfenced pasture needed an unlimited supply of men of low mental calibre, content to lead lives of brutish loneliness as they tended the flocks. Later, too, I would observe that shepherding is not the pretty and romantic occupation dwelt upon by poets and the creators of Dresden figurines. Still, all this was in my future, and now, baffled as to why I had been brought here to this house where no one showed more than a passing interest in myself, I eased some of my frustrations by sketching.

It was my one real talent, and having fortunately brought my drawing things with me, I took every opportunity to go out into the gardens and find a suitable subject for my pencil. At least, for a while, I could forget the humiliation of my position, penniless and unwanted in a strange land where the natives seemed as cold as the winds.

Unlike more conventionally brought up young girls, I had never slaved long hours under the watchful eye of a drawing master, but had received lessons from time to time from my father's artistic friends.

'No, not like that!' one would say, taking the crayon from my hand. 'See, do this, and you'll get the perspective.'

Or:

'Be firm. Don't dilly dally. People want to see what you're doing.' And again, the crayon would be taken away and sharp lines drawn where I had been too timorous to make more than feeble marks.

It was rough and ready tuition, given with the assumption that I could do it if shown how.

One afternoon, while I was assiduously attempting to transfer a row of formally clipped yews to paper, a shadow fell across my work. I looked up, startled, to see my grandfather, leaning on the cane he needed to walk any distance. Without a word, he took the pad, and inspected my sketch.

'You draw well,' he said, drily.

'Thank you, sir,' I answered, meekly. I had studied those glum volumes left on my night table, out of the sheer desperation of having nothing else to do, and it was slowly coming to me that a meek manner was appreciated in the English female, and my instinct for self preservation was urging me to cultivate it, on the surface, anyway.

My pad was handed back to me, and I expected him to continue on his walk. Conversations with my grandfather were always of the two-sentence variety. He said something, and I answered, and that was the end of it.

'How did my son die?'

It was unexpected, and a shock to me to realise that, as with Mrs Birrell, he had not been told the truth.

'Come on, girl, I want to know. Was it in a drunken brawl?'

Yet, even as he asked the question, I knew, with a flash of wisdom beyond my years, that he wanted to be reassured. Harsh, proud and grasping he was, and undoubtedly embittered by the way in which my father had gone out of his way to run headlong against his family's wishes, but he was an old man, and a father who had outlived his own three children. Power was in my possession at that instant, the power to hurt and gain some passing satisfaction, by telling him that his son had been slaughtered because of his association with a trollop. As I hesitated, my grandfather spoke again.

'I was told that he was stabbed to death by an unknown assailant.'

'He was murdered by a madman.' Yes, that was what the intruder had been, a madman. Who else would have committed such a crime on behalf of a woman like Antoinette?

'How did it happen?'

'The man broke into our villa. That's all. It was all over, very quickly.'

I think my grandfather guessed that I was keeping the exact truth from him, but after looking down into my face, he sighed and shook his head.

'There must be a curse on my blood. Three children, and all dead by violence. Frederick at Badajoz, Franklin's mother and father in a boating accident, and now your father.'

The all too familiar flutter of fear passed through me. Was this the real meaning of the witch's words, that I was one of an accursed family?

My grandfather continued talking.

'You look like Frederick. More like him than your father. You don't resemble *her* at all.'

By 'her' I knew that he meant my mother, and I did not feel that it was altogether a compliment to be told that I resembled an uncle. After all, I had my share of feminine pride. He qualified his statement after a pause.

'Frederick was almost girlish looking as a

youth. But he grew into a brave man.' My grandfather sighed again. 'Your father wanted to join Wellington's army when Bonaparte escaped from Elba, but I forbade it. I had my heart set on a seat in the House of Commons for Will. He had as many opportunities as Robert Peel, but he chose to go to the devil instead. I've often wondered whether a spell of action in the army might've cured him of his wildness.'

Now that the old man had broken the ice, he seemed to want to confide in me.

'Frederick's wife was a fool, of course. She kept the girls with her too long. Spoiled their chances.'

Then, he seemed to repent of having said so much and continued on his way for a few yards, leaning quite heavily on his cane. Suddenly, he spoke again, over his shoulder.

'Your half-brothers are expected home tomorrow.'

This news left me in considerable trepidation. Mrs Furlong loathed me. She had never once addressed a word to me; but again and again, I had caught her looking at me with a hatred so fierce that her eyes glittered with it. The fluttery spinsters went their own way — they were actually in their thirties still, but looked older — and Franklin had not forgiven me

53

for the way in which I had rebuffed him. What, then, could I expect from my half-brothers? Would they side actively with their mother, or would they obey their father's injunction to care for me?

They arrived late the following day, and I watched nervously from a window as they alighted from the carriage, followed by another young man a few years older than they, and dressed more soberly than my brothers. Franklin, who had returned home earlier than usual, had come quietly into the library, and spoke to me from behind, unexpectedly, making me jump.

'Look at that fine pair,' he muttered savagely. 'Coming home to breathe a bit of our vulgar northern air before going off on their Grand Tour. They have to be turned into fine gentlemen. I had to learn to run the business so that they could be supported and move up into the aristocracy. They're the sons of a son, you see, Clytie. I'm only the son of a daughter who married beneath herself.'

I felt considerable astonishment as he spoke, and sorry for him at the same time. I disliked Franklin, but for that little while we had something in common. We were the less desirable members of the family.

'Which one is which?' I asked.

'The taller one is Tom, the fair one is Horace. The odd man out is Charles Ellett, their watchdog. He's studying for the church.'

Then he slid his unbearable paw about my waist, in a gesture which was half conspiratorial, half amorous.

'A lot depends on Tom and Horace taking to you,' he said, and as I moved away, I saw the worried, yet speculative expression in his protuberant grey eyes. 'If they like you and decide to do their duty by you — when they attain their majorities, of course — remember who brought you to them.'

'All I want,' I replied, dramatically, 'is to forget you.'

'Puss puss,' chided Franklin. 'Believe me, my child, we should work together. *I* don't want to find myself out in the cold. *You* need to make your way in life.'

'If I had the fare I'd go straight back to Mrs Birrell,' I stated, with a show of confidence I did not feel. 'I can make my own way in life.'

'Don't be stupid, Clytie. You need to stay in the good graces of the Furlongs as much as I do. You're a pretty child, but without the Furlongs behind you, you've no hope of making any sort of a match. I'll sing your praises to your brothers, but I want you to remember I'm your friend.'

'I'd sooner be friends with a spider,' I declared, and he laughed in that grating way of his, not the jolly hearty laugh one would have expected from this corpulent man, but a sort of snigger.

'Go and pretty yourself up,' he ordered, and because I wanted to be free of him and now felt too upset to chance meeting my brothers as they entered the house, I ran upstairs to my own little room. There I sat for quite an hour, conscious of the merry male voices and laughter which had invaded this sombre house. I plucked up the courage once to peep out of my door and called out to a passing servant that I had a headache and would like to eat off a tray in my room if that would not be too much bother. The place for a family skeleton on such an occasion, I decided, wallowing in self pity, was safely locked away in a cupboard.

Not five minutes later, there was a brisk tap on that same door, and the butler informed me in his usual lordly fashion that the master awaited me in the library.

I checked my appearance hastily, licking a forefinger to smooth my eyebrows, and twisted my unruly blonde curls back into the ringlets into which I had dressed them earlier that day. Then, with an impulsive attempt at defiance, remembering the disfavour which had greeted my silver cross, I took it out and fastened it about my neck. After this, I pulled myself up very erect, and descended the main staircase, brushing against Mrs Furlong on the way. She sent me her usual look of complete detestation, and I took a deep breath to calm my nerves.

The library seemed full of men. Grandfather stood in his habitual place before the fireplace — the day was mild, but as was usual except on the very warmest days, there was a fire, to keep the air dry and warm for the books, I was told — and my cousin Franklin lounged to one side. He gave a slight but very meaning nod in my direction, and I pretended to ignore him. My half-brothers arose from their chairs as I entered, and I saw, out of the corner of my eye, their 'watchdog,' Mr Ellett, standing near the window, ostensibly gazing out at the gardens.

When he saw me, he immediately excused himself, and as he passed me, he sent me a half smile. Why, I thought, he's a very handsome young man. He stood just under six feet, had dark glossy hair coming down on to his cheeks in fashionable side whiskers, and unexpectedly merry dark hazel eyes under well-marked black brows. Used to Italian custom, I had to adjust a little to the idea that most English clergymen were eligible as husbands.

'So you're our little sister!'

It was Horace who spoke, and as he came towards me with an extended hand, I felt an instant liking for this youth who so resembled myself in our mutual fairness. Tom, on the other hand, was more diffident. He liked to size people up before committing himself, and at this stage, I think that my existence still embarrassed him.

'Yes,' said our grandfather, brutally, 'this is the young woman who has been left into your mutual care by your brainless scallywag of a father.'

'Don't take any notice. His bark is worse than his bite,' said Horace, cheerfully. 'Come and sit down. We're off to Italy ourselves next week, to further our education, and I daresay you can give us some advice.'

Yet, in spite of this friendliness, I ate my dinner alone in my room. No one insisted that I come down, for my presence at the feast would have been an irritation. Afterwards, making sure first that the coast was clear, I crept down to the library to find myself a book, and it was whilst I was choosing a volume that I became aware that there was someone else in the room.

It was Mr Ellett, out of my first sight in a deep chair.

'Good evening,' he said, smiling again at me.

'H — hullo.' One would have thought, after those free and easy years in Naples when I had conversed with men many years my senior on all sorts of topics, that I should have been more at ease. But father's middle-aged friends were one thing. This handsome young man was another.

'Are you feeling better?'

In time, I remembered that I had had a headache, and said that I was a little improved, and all the while I knew that he did not believe in my headache.

'I was thinking,' he said, 'that I would enjoy a game of draughts. But it needs two to play.'

This invitation was irresistible, and we settled ourselves to play. I think he beat me twice, and as I was gaining mastery in the third game, he sat back in his chair, solemn faced.

'Your position here isn't happy, is it?' he asked, directly.

'No,' I said, dolefully. 'I didn't have a headache, you know.'

'Yes, I knew. Well, I'm in much the same position.' He grinned merrily. 'No one quite knows what to do with me on these occasions. I try to make myself inconspicuous.'

I managed a laugh, too, and thought, I would like to marry someone like Mr Ellett.

'I'd like to help if I could.' It became less exciting as he continued. 'That is my mission in life, Miss Clytie. Helping others.'

'I want to go back to London,' I confessed, and then told him about Mrs Birrell, and how my cousin Franklin had taken me from her kindly protection and had brought me here. Now I was trapped, simply because I did not have the money for the fare back to London.

'I'll talk to your brothers about it.' He moved one of the draughts, expertly taking two of mine. 'They're very young, and you must realise that they're likely to consider their mother's feelings before yours. Still, I'll do what I can to make them understand your situation. Now, let's continue our game.'

He won, of course, but I went off to bed with the pleasantly warm feeling that I had found a friend.

Over the next few days, I saw little of Tom and Horace, for they were off on a round of visiting friends and entertaining in return. Franklin kept urging me to try harder to win their esteem, and I could only reply that I seldom had the opportunity to exchange more than a few words with them.

'But, you're making an impression on the parson, aren't you?' Franklin treated me to one of his leers. 'Not such a bad idea, by half, little cousin. *They* like him.'

I must have blushed, because he uttered that repellant snigger of his. 'And you, too, or I'm a Dutchman.'

'Oh, be quiet,' I retorted, and if I had been in Italy, I would have used one of Serafina's stronger expressions.

Mr Ellett found time to walk with me in the gardens during the day before my brothers and he were to leave for their extended tour of the Continent. My sixteen and three-quarter year old heart was beating so hard under my demure grey bodice that I felt sure that he must hear its throb if he could not see its palpitation, but Mr Ellett, alas, still looked upon me as a case in need of help.

'I've spoken to your brothers,' he told me, 'and they're talking to your grandfather now about the desirability of your return to London. In truth, Miss Clytie — ' he always called me that, mainly, I think, to overcome the difficulty of calling me Furlong when I was really Starling — 'you'd be wise to leave here as soon as possible.'

'I'd like to,' I said, candidly, pretending to admire a rosebud as we passed. 'My cousin, Mr Parker, brought me here, and I know that he's only looking out for himself.'

Charles Ellett stopped walking and faced me. For a long time, I enshrined in my memory how he looked at that moment, with his fine eyes robbed of their merriment, and his good looking face very serious.

'I don't know what is in your cousin's mind,' he said, 'but it wasn't his idea that you should come here. It was Mrs Furlong's. She hates you. If she has the chance, she'll do her best to ruin your life. Perhaps I'm exceeding my duty by telling you this, but please heed my warning, for your own sake.'

For some seconds, I was speechless, and yet, now that I could think about it in perspective, I could see that he was probably right. My grandfather had seemed nonplussed at the time of my arrival, and Franklin Parker had, when he had collected me in London, given no real reason as to why I was required at Furlong Hall.

I had no chance that evening to confront Franklin, for he was out late, and in the morning the house was in confusion. Franklin was leaving for London with my brothers and

Mr Ellett, to present yet another petition to his member on the subject of transportation to New South Wales. Before they left, both Tom and Horace expressed their pleasure at having met me, and Horace hugged me quite affectionately, and told me that he was looking forward to seeing me on their return, and that he would write to me regularly.

Mr Ellett shook hands with me warmly, and told me to remain cheerful, and then, to my astonishment, I felt him press something hard and cold into my palm. Before I could utter a word, he had hurried outside, and as Mrs Furlong was on the terrace waiting to bid farewell to her sons, I preferred to stay indoors and not follow. When I looked down at my hand, I saw therein five golden sovereigns. I knew what they were for — my fare back to London — and I was at once grateful and ashamed. Mr Ellett was not rich, and I was angry with myself for playing on his feelings to an extent that he felt obliged to help me.

As I stared at the coins, wondering what to do, Franklin materialised at my elbow, all dressed up for travelling, and looking fatter and more pompous than ever.

'What have you there?' he demanded suspiciously.

'My fare back to London,' I said, seizing

this opportunity of putting him back into his box.

'I see you've been working on that soft-headed parson. Well, you don't need your fare back to anywhere, little cousin. Our lawyer is coming this morning to see our grandfather about your future.' He gave my shoulders a quick squeeze, and I drew away. 'Now remember all I've told you, and for heavens' sake be pleasant to Grandfather.'

'Franklin!' I was not going to let him go, without delving deeper. 'Who told you to bring me here to Furlong Hall? It was Mrs Furlong, wasn't it?'

He looked uncomfortable, and bit at his plump lower lip.

'Perhaps, in a way. Still, it's working out well for you, little cousin.'

'*You are a toad*!' I said it very slowly, and with all the loathing I could muster.

'And you, little cousin, are a charming wildcat.' He kissed me messily on the cheek, and then bounced off before I could administer the slap he deserved. 'Be a good girl while I'm gone,' he added over his wide coat collar as he hurried out to the carriage.

I went upstairs, found my drawing things, and escaped into the grounds for the rest of the morning. When I returned, called

64

back by hunger, with my hair windblown and my nose slightly sunburnt, for in my fit of temper I had neglected to take my hat, I was told that my grandfather wished to see me, immediately.

He was in his study, alone, seated at his secretaire, and as I entered, he indicated that he wished me to sit in the stiff-backed chair by the window.

'Where have you been? You look a regular hoyden.' He did not allow me to answer, but continued talking in this angry fashion. 'Well, your brothers seem to have taken a liking to you, though looking at you now it's hard to understand why. I've discussed the matter with our lawyer, and it's to be arranged that you'll receive a small part of the income which will come to them when they attain their majorities. But before that, you'll be sent off somewhere to cultivate a few airs and graces.'

'Can't I go back to Mrs Birrell?' I asked.

'Sophie's? Nothing against her, but you'll end up looking after her in her old age. Horace is going in for law, you know. Always keen on it. That fool Franklin thinks I want Horace to take over from him. Uh! Whoever heard of a factory manager being raised to the peerage. Still, while he thinks that way, he'll toe the line. Both the boys have their heads screwed on, more than could be said for your idiot of a father. Horace'll be happy to have you with him when he sets up an establishment of his own, but that's in the future. You could be married before then. In the meantime, we'll have to find a finishing school that has a good reputation and'll take you. Now, don't glare at me like that, girl. You've landed on your feet, and you ought to be thankful.'

'But I am.' I found my voice, wanting to pinch myself to make sure that I was not dreaming. 'I — I thought to be a governess, sir. I didn't expect . . .'

If Mrs Furlong thought to do me harm by bringing me here, I thought, still dazed, she had made a mistake, and at the same time, I wondered how I could send back Mr Ellett's money.

Grandfather had taken up his cane, and rising to his feet, he pointed to a picture on the wall.

'Thank the lucky chance which made you look like her,' he said, grumpily, and I gazed up at the painting. It was of a young lady, my grandmother before her marriage, very much in the Gainsborough style of softly flowing skirts, artlessly arranged curls, and a large hat held so carelessly that one could hardly suspect that it was part of the pose. My own face looked back at me in the style of long ago, so different from my own corkscrew ringlets, which always fell to pieces within the hour, and my stiffly fashioned dresses.

Then I was dismissed, curtly, and a thousand times that day I had to convince myself that it was true. Undisciplined though I had been for most of my life, I did not mind the thought of finishing school, for there I could meet other girls of my own age, and perhaps make friends and be accepted for myself. I even sent up a few little prayers that my poor father could know how well things were turning out for me. I regretted not going back to Mrs Birrell, but if the school was in London, I would be able to visit her from time to time. It was a happy day, and not the least part of the pleasure was in the knowledge that I would soon be away from Franklin's slimy advances.

I was soon to have my dream shattered. Fresh tragedy was almost upon me, the disaster which was to lead me ultimately into the clutches of the unscrupulous and scheming Quentin, alias Foxy, Lambert.

6

I had gone downstairs to find a book, and was emerging from the library when I heard a sound at the head of the stairs. Glancing up into the dimness, I saw my grandfather stagger, lose his balance, and fall down the top flight. In but a moment, I had cried out and had run up to assist him. He was groaning, and if I had known more of medicine, I should have recognised that he had suffered a stroke, for one side of his face was pale and the other flushed. Now servants appeared, and on the landing above me, Mrs Furlong, and as I looked up at her, I realised the cause of those days spent shut away in her room. She had been drinking heavily, and now appeared unsteady and dishevelled, as well as sounding slurred of speech.

Grandfather's personal servant ran down to us, and ordered a footman to send someone for the doctor immediately, and I tried to explain what had happened.

'You scheming little slut!' It was my father's widow, and these were the first words she had ever addressed to me. 'You pushed him. I saw you! You know he's changed his will to give you what you don't deserve, and you wanted him dead. You pushed him.'

The shy spinsters had emerged from their own apartment, and were hovering nervously in the background, while it seemed that the hallway downstairs was filled with Furlong Hall's huge staff, all gaping and listening.

'But I was downstairs!' I cried. 'He did fall. I saw him.'

'And I saw you!' Her thin finger was pointed down at me as I stood there helplessly. 'You were standing behind him, right where I am now, and you pushed him. I knew you were evil the moment you came into this house. Evil, evil! You're as evil and lost as your wicked father.'

Her voice ranted on and on, until her own maid took her by the arm. Then I ran to my own room, and shut the door, trembling and sobbing. My grandfather was dying, and I was to be accused of his murder. What the fortune teller had told me throbbed in my head. Everywhere I went there was death, violent death. I was accused, and who would believe me when Mrs Furlong had denounced me so strongly?

I gathered up a bundle of what I thought I would need, and without stopping to think stole out of the house down the back stairs and through a rear door, just as the doctor

69

arrived in his gig. I climbed over a wall so that the gatekeeper would not see me, and began walking. It was full moon, and fairly warm, and, used to roaming the steep paths near my Naples home, I was well able to walk a considerable distance without much effort. In time, I came upon a canal, and whilst wondering what direction to take so as to find a bridge, another thought struck me. What better way to move out of the district than on one of the barges below?

There is no need to dwell upon my wanderings over the next month. All that needs to be explained is that, when my money was exhausted and the few shillings obtained from the sale of my silver cross spent, I found myself standing before a group of gentlemen known collectively as a Board of Guardians. It was a memorable day, my seventeenth birthday, when it was to be duly decided whether my ragged, half-starved self should be installed in the workhouse, there to expiate my sin of becoming so poor.

I answered their questions in a low voice, and one of them leaned back and regarded me in a puzzled fashion.

'You talk like an educated young woman,' he accused me. 'Have you no relatives who would take you in?'

I shook my head, numb with fear. In my

mind's eye, I could visualise, as I had during so many wretched nights spent trying to rest in a variety of makeshift shelters, myself being dragged to the gallows for murder, or left in prison to rot for the rest of my life.

There was some twittering and whispering amidst the Guardians, those well fed gentlemen who decided the fate of persons foolish enough to allow themselves to become so destitute that they needed to apply to enter those temples of no-hope, the workhouses.

'Miss Starling,' said one of the men, calling me by the name I had given to throw any possible pursuers off the trail, 'there is an alternative to the workhouse.'

I gave a little nod of the head to show that I was listening, and he cleared his throat before continuing.

'We are despatching a number of young — um — female persons from Liverpool to New South Wales. There is a shortage of women in the colony, and you would be better employed there than in the workhouse.'

I had not yet heard the New South Wales expression, 'Sydney or the bush', meaning one choice being as bad as the other. I weighed the miseries of life in the workhouse against the chances of being drowned or dying of fever on the way to New South

71

Wales, and decided on the latter.

So, on a slow old tub called a 'bride ship' by the wits, myself and twenty-three other young women crossed the world to Australia. We were of two kinds, poor but decent girls who hoped to make a better life for themselves, and debauched and depraved young creatures who were not quite wicked enough for gaol. We former banded ourselves together, and happily one of the first class passengers (who were mostly horrified, of course, to find themselves travelling on a 'bride ship') took an interest in us. She was already domiciled in New South Wales, and was returning there after settling her sons at school in England. It was thanks to her that some of the extreme tedium of the voyage was eased for those of us who had to suffer the cramped and primitive conditions 'tween decks.

She arranged little classes, sorting us into groups of those who were literate, could sew, or possessed other skills which could be taught to others who lacked them. I took my first lessons in simple needlework, for my father, while teaching me to sort out the Caesars, had never bothered to ensure that I could sew on a button. Our mentor also spoke to us about New South Wales. She warned us against the crude and violent men we could meet there, and told us to be very careful before undertaking marriage. As well, she gave us another piece of sound advice.

There was in Sydney a woman, a Mrs Chisholm, who had our interests truly at heart. She devoted most of her time and energy to seeing that newly arrived immigrant girls received fair treatment and were placed in suitable employment. Thanks to her efforts, many girls who had landed in Sydney almost penniless and in such a hopeless state of heart that they otherwise would have become prostitutes, had found a safe niche in society. If by some chance, we were not met at the quay by Mrs Chisholm or one of her helpers, we must seek her out without delay.

Eventually, after all the tensions and spells of appalling weather when we were sure that we would all perish, we sailed through a break in the rocky coastline into Port Jackson, quite unprepared for the beauty of this huge harbour with its many bays and inlets. Even our incorrigibles, whose senses had been stunted since childhood by poverty and gin, stood on the deck expressing, in the crudest of jargon, their wonder at the loveliness of this place under clear blue skies. Sydney itself was small and frequently squalid, although there were some fine houses to be glimpsed through the trees which grew almost to the water's edge away from the town itself.

Our ship was berthed in Sydney Cove itself, the place where the first settlers had landed just over a half century previously. To one side was a headland surmounted by a small fort, in front a collection of warehouses, sheds, and government offices with streets running up the slopes behind, and forming the other arm of the arc, a steep incline upon which was built an ugly jumble of huts and cottages. The whole town was thus, a collection of quite good buildings mixed in with the makeshift. For me, there was something of Italy in the clear sunlight and the heat beating down on to the dusty streets, but; whereas Italy had the charms of its many centuries of civilisation, all I could see here was raw and new.

Yet, I did not wish to be reminded of Italy and the terror of All Hallows' Eve, any more than I wanted to remember my disastrous sojourn at Furlong Hall. However, even as I tried to shut the past from my mind, homesickness washed through me. I should have been glad to have been able to step ashore from this little ship which had been prison for so many months, but I had the feeling that once I carried my small bundle of belongings ashore, I would be separated from the past forever.

As our friend had promised, we were taken under Mrs Chisholm's wing, and suitable places of employment found for us. Some of the girls, who had had no thought during the long voyage except to revert to their old ways, scurried off immediately to the purlieus of Sydney, but amongst these poor dregs, there were those who were determined to make good. On their own, they would have failed, but with that remarkable woman to help them, they were soon safely settled. She spoke to each of us, and for me there was an especially keen glance.

Caroline Chisholm was then in her early forties, and her bright red hair was losing its lustre, but the lovely blue eyes shone with their owner's intelligence and dedication of purpose.

'I believe you're better educated than the other girls,' she stated, and she waited for some moments, as if expecting me to explain. I said nothing.

'Well, Miss Starling, educated, well-spoken young women are a rarity amongst assisted immigrant girls. Do you think you could be a governess?'

How strange. I had planned to be a

governess before my stay at Furlong Hall changed my destiny. I nodded.

'Very well.' She smiled. 'Did you run away from home, Miss Starling?'

I remained mute, and when she understood that I was not going to confide in her, she wrote something opposite my name on a list.

'You do bear the most amazing resemblance to a lady I know here in Sydney,' she said, then. 'Perhaps you are related?'

'Oh no,' I said hastily. 'I'm sure that I have no relatives in New South Wales.'

Vaguely, I recalled that the Furlongs had some interests in Australia, and the thought of having my identity revealed frightened me very much.

'I have an excellent position for you,' Mrs Chisholm continued. 'It is on a very well established farm some distance from Sydney. Remember, Miss Starling, I have to place my trust in you.'

'Oh, I'll do my best,' I assured her. 'I shall, Mrs Chisholm. I — I want to be settled somewhere.'

These last words came from the bottom of my heart. I was not by nature footloose. I wanted security. I wished more than anything that I should find a place where I belonged, where I could forget my father's murder and my poor grandfather's accident.

Two years later, it seemed that I had found my security. I had settled in quite well with the Reeds. They had a large property, partly farmed and partly grazed, near the Hawkesbury River to the northwest of Sydney. They were wealthy people, with other property in the colony, and grazing leases besides over the Blue Mountains and far to the south in the Port Phillip district. They had already built a well-planned and large house to replace the sprawling cottage which had been the original owner's home, and as the gardens were being planted with choice imported trees, the place had the beginnings of a graciousness not often found in New South Wales. My charges varied in number up to about a dozen, depending on the families of those currently employed near the house, and to cope with this, I used a small school room built on its own in the grounds.

I liked being a teacher, and adapted fairly well to my new surroundings. Although, in accordance with the general practice of most settlers, the land about had been stripped of much of its original vegetation, there were still pockets of bushland left within easy distance, so that I could employ my pencil and pad in picturing some of the strange trees, and more occasionally, animals and birds. By far the most unpleasant feature of life here, I soon discovered, was a varied and extremely active insect population. Large creatures soon vanished before the white man's onslaught, but the lesser species seemed positively to thrive. There forever seemed to be a line of ants marching towards food, or a cloud of flies waiting to alight upon one's dinner, or a large and evil spider lurking on the ceiling, or a dozen fierce mosquitoes to be chased out from beneath one's net canopy before one could sleep. These were, of course, apart from the roaches, beetles, grubs, moths and termites which abounded in their myriads. Before one sat anywhere out of doors, one always inspected, and if practicable, lifted and squashed beforehand.

It was no wonder that visitors complained about the trivial quality of conversation amidst the ladies of New South Wales 'society.' All their time, apart from a sort of running war against indifferent and intemperate servants, was spent fighting insect invaders.

As I neared my twentieth birthday, I became engaged to be married to a young man called James Harkness who had formerly managed one of the Reeds' inland stations.

Soon after we had made up our minds to marry, he was sent south to their Port Phillip run. I missed him terribly, and longed for the letter which would tell me to join him, but Mrs Reed made it quite clear that she resented losing her governess.

Mrs Reed was not a difficult person to have as an employer, but like many of the colonial 'gentry,' she had come from an ordinary background, for which she compensated by developing a most lofty opinion of her own importance. Remembering as I did the easy manners of my father and his friends, many of whom may have been wastrels but still boasted some of the noblest blood of Britain in their veins, I found the careful pretensions of Mrs Reed and her set somewhat extraordinary. However, she was generally considerate, and I was surprised when she spoke to me sharply about my sad looks since Jem Harkness had left.

'Miss Starling! I must ask you to pull yourself together. My husband planned months ago to send Mr Harkness to Port Phillip. It will do no harm for you to have time to think it over.'

'But my mind is quite made up, Mrs Reed,' I replied, astounded at her bluntness.

Mrs Reed, who had visited me at the

school room after lessons had ended for the day, picked up a primer and flicked through it. Then she glanced at the wall where I had pinned my own sketches of various objects to implement the limited material contained in the primers. To make lessons more interesting for my young pupils, who were frequently the native-born children of convict labourers, I had drawn such things as parrots, kangaroos, emus, lizards, and other creatures more familiar to them than badgers, jackdaws and the like.

'You're a very gifted young woman, Miss Starling,' she said curtly. 'Don't throw yourself away.'

I watched her back resentfully as she walked across the garden to the house. I was the best teacher she was likely to find to fit in with her schemes for educating everyone who fell within her net. It was obvious why she did not want to lose me to James Harkness. Who else would stay in this out of the way place, far from amusements and town distractions, for my small wages and keep?

The following Sunday afternoon I still brooded over Mrs Reed's remarks. I was very much in love — how absurd my childish feelings for Charles Ellett seemed now — and no amount of persuasion was going to change my intention of becoming Mrs Harkness at the very first opportunity. I had gone out into the grounds to indulge my passion for drawing, all the time rather guiltily aware that I should have been stitching at an article useful for my married life. Although the scene stretching in front of me, green lands falling away to the river flats, was quite pleasing, I was drawing from memory some Roman ruins to use in a history lesson.

Mrs Reed had continued harping on the matter of my talents. She said that it was a shame I was not a little older. I was a born teacher, and, if I had been thirty instead of twenty, she and some other ladies would have gladly sponsored the opening of a school for girls with myself in charge.

Unfortunately, my sketching was interrupted by the splash of a raindrop on my pad. It had fallen from a cloud which had crept up to cover the sun while I was pondering over the injustice of being parted from my lover and at the same time being subjected to Mrs Reed's nagging. I was all too familiar with these showers. What the locals called a 'good sprinkle of rain' would have passed for a deluge elsewhere.

Therefore, I gathered together my things, and scurried towards the house. Mrs Reed had taken her children out to a neighbour's house for a birthday party, and I felt decidedly disgruntled at having my few precious private hours stolen in this way.

Near the house, I heard hoofbeats, and as I ran to beat the shower, I saw a thickset, well-dressed man riding towards our stable yard. He was a fellow landowner and fellow magistrate of Mr Reed's, and he lost no time in following me into the house, because I had barely reached the top of the stairs when I heard him address Mr Reed, who had come from his study to greet his friend.

'Filthy weather,' grumbled the visitor. 'Edgar, I rode up from Sydney this morning, and I came straightaway to get to the bottom of it.'

An instinct made me pause and listen.

'This governess of yours, pretty little fair thing. Miss Starling, she calls herself. Ain't her Christian name Clytie? Outlandish name. Never heard of it before, not as a girl's name anyway. There's an enquiry out about a Miss Clytie Furlong. Very fair, small, about twenty years old, has a very slight Italian accent. I've noticed the way that governess of yours talks. Not quite English.'

'Miss Starling? Why? I'm sure she hasn't done anything wrong.'

'There's a real brou-ha-ha about it, Edgar. The Governor himself has been approached

82

over it. A family called Furlong . . . '

I waited to hear no more, but ran to my room. Closing the door, I stood irresolute for some moments, caught by that dreadful turmoil of feeling that had seized me on the night when Mrs Furlong had accused me of attempted murder. I'll go to Jem, I thought. He'll know what to do. My little store of money hardly seemed adequate for the coach fare to Sydney, the first step in the journey to Melbourne, and besides, waiting until tomorrow morning for the coach was hardly practicable under the circumstances. Out of my window I could see two things which, added together, gave me an inspiration. One was a washline, beneath a veranda, bearing a number of men's dungaree garments, the usual clothes of working men in those parts, and the other was the magistrate's horse, under shelter, but still saddled.

It was a crazy scheme, but I knew that I had to act quickly, and as a start, I grabbed my scissors and chopped my hair short. Then, snatching up a few odds and ends into a bundle, I bolted out of a back door, hearing Mr Reed's voice calling out to me upstairs. I whipped what I needed off that line, and in another minute was mounted and urging the surprised horse towards the front gate of the homestead property. Fear does wonderful things, for I had hardly ever ridden before in my life, except on donkeys as a child, but now yells from behind me added to my panic.

Furiously, I cantered along, hanging on for dear life, for about two miles, when I half dismounted and half fell from the saddle, and changed into my stolen clothing, hiding my own in a wombat's hole beneath some bushes. The absolute enormity of what I had done was beginning to strike me. I had stolen a magistrate's horse. The notorious Women's Factory at Parramatta would be my fate if I did not keep a clear head. Therefore, I took the reins of that placid horse, which was eyeing me in a bemused and reproachful fashion, and fastened them to a sapling at the side of the track. I could hear my pursuers not so very far behind, and I knew that the beast would soon be found.

Then I ran off into some scrubby bushland, in what I hoped was the direction of Sydney.

7

I had no intention of telling Mr Lambert my life story, and still less of explaining how I had come to Sydney perched uncomfortably amongst a cart load of vegetables. My every instinct told me to be on my guard against him. Therefore, in reply to his demand that I tell him the truth about myself, I repeated that my motive in attempting to stow away was to reach Melbourne and my fiancé.

'Ah, your fiancé.' Mr Lambert pounced upon this. 'Well, it's as good an excuse as any.'

'I've almost no money, and he — he expects me.'

That was half true. Jem did expect me, eventually.

'I wonder if he's getting what he expected.' Mr Lambert did not even try to hide the contempt in his voice as he regarded my scarecrow figure.

I knew quite well that Jem would be as amazed as anyone to see me looking like this, but Mr Lambert's open sneer angered me. I may not have been on the same level, socially, as the Reeds, but most of the gossip which circulated amongst their friends reached me sooner or later. No man earned the nickname of Foxy by being upright and straightforward. Or so said the Reeds, who had discussed him thoroughly some months previously when his wife had been lost, presumed drowned, during a shipwreck off the southern coast of New South Wales.

Many of the colony's instant fortunes had collapsed during the recent depression, but Foxy Lambert was the one who bought up land when prices were at their lowest after the collapse, and took up the debts of others when they reached the point of despair. Foxy in looks and foxy by nature, he had earned his unpleasant soubriquet.

As I tried to think of something crushing to say, Mr Lambert sauntered forward, and around me, inspecting me.

'Where did you get those clothes?' he demanded. 'They don't fit. Even the poorest dungaree settler'd be more particular than that. I suppose you stole them.'

I could not answer this, so I gave a little sniff to show what I thought of his accusation. Once again, that thoughtful look was resting on his face.

'What else did you steal? Not your shoes. They seem to fit. You should have remembered your shoes, Miss Smith. I saw straight away that they were a woman's.'

'I'm no thief. Well, I did borrow a horse,' I amended, under his unrelenting and unspeakably cynical gaze. 'But they would have found it easily enough.'

'And who are they? The people you're assigned to?'

'Assigned! I'm a free settler, Mr Lambert.'

If he recognised the barb, he gave no sign, but returned to his desk and opened a drawer. I half expected a pistol or something similar, but he withdrew a cigar, which he lit at a small lamp kept burning on a corner of his desk, probably as much for this purpose as for softening sealing wax.

'And as a free settler, what did you do for *they*? Scrub floors? Make the butter? Drink all their liquor as soon as they were out of the house?'

He blew out a cloud of smoke, which made the atmosphere in that nasty little room even stuffier, and I suppressed my need to cough.

'I was the governess,' I hissed, clenching my fists.

He laughed, incredulously, taking in my chopped hair and shapeless dungarees again.

'Governess!' He sucked on his cigar and another noxious cloud wafted into the air. 'You don't expect me to believe that.' Then he became grave again. 'If I had a scrap of sense, I'd turn you over to the law. With my record, I could be charged with harbouring for merely having you here in my office. But I'd be a fool to let this chance slip me by.'

'Oh?' I asked.

'You and I, Miss Smith, are going to strike a bargain.'

'No,' I declared, taking a step backwards.

'You'd best hear me out. And there's no need to look so outraged. I'm not interested in your — um — virtue, if you have any. Sit down.'

I sat down, so angry that I was past words, but at the same time realising that I had little alternative except to listen to what this unpleasant man had to say. As he walked to his own chair behind his desk, I observed him again, and in more detail. He was not a large person, being perhaps five or six inches taller than myself, but with a lithe way of moving which hinted at a well-knit, if slender, body under the well-tailored clothes. At twenty, I tended to think of anyone past thirty as elderly, but I placed his age at somewhere between that of James's twenty-eight and my late father's forty-five at the time of his death. Mr Lambert, I discovered later, was in fact thirty-four at this time, so that my guess was fairly accurate.

He sat, apparently lost in thought, for some minutes without saying a word, and at the end of it, he thumped his right fist on the top of the desk.

'And I'll give you a hundred pounds at the end of it,' he announced. 'It'd be worth it.'

'What would?' I asked, not liking my feeling of being drawn deep into a quicksand.

'I want you to help me find my wife.'

My puzzlement must have shown plainly, because he began to explain, and as he spoke, I wished that I had remained to answer the magistrate's questions.

'Miss Smith, I want you to look at the map up here on the wall.'

Obediently, still not quite comprehending, I watched as he once more sprung to his feet and pointed to the south-eastern corner of New South Wales, where the coastline turned to the west and formed the northern shore of that wild stretch of water called the Bass Straits, separating the continent from Tasmania, or Van Diemen's Land as it was then.

'Five months ago,' he began, 'my wife visited her father, Mr Eldridge, here in Launceston.' He indicated a spot on the northern shore of Tasmania as he talked. 'Then, on the way back to Sydney, the ship in which she was travelling was hit by heavy seas and foundered here.'

His forefinger rested on a spot some distance past that western turn.

'This is about a hundred and seventy miles due east of the settlement at Melbourne, which is here, on Port Phillip Bay. The ship came to grief along the Ninety Mile Beach, off Gipps Land. The area is very wild, with no good harbour. Are you listening, Miss Smith?'

I nodded, obediently, thinking that Mr Lambert would have made a good school master.

'This region was unexplored until about five years ago, when it was entered from the north here through the ranges, by a Scots cattleman named Angus McMillan, who called it Caledonia Australis, after his native land. Shortly afterwards, the Polish explorer, Count Strezlecki crossed this Gipps Land through extremely difficult country, and reached Melbourne. He named it after our Governor, Sir George Gipps, and has gained most of the credit for its discovery.'

He glanced at me, to make sure that I was absorbing this geography lesson, and it may seem odd, but I knew less of this land where I resided than of the world as a whole.

'Mr McMillan continued his explorations, and here, at the western end of the Ninety

Mile Beach, sheltered from the worst of the Bass Straits' gales by a string of islands, he found a safe anchorage. About the same time, the steamer *Clonmel* was wrecked on one of the islands off shore, and while waiting for rescue to reach them from Melbourne, some members of the crew selected the site of what is now Port Albert. This, Miss Smith, is the sole access to Gipps Land, and the only way goods can leave or enter. Although many cattle runs have been taken up, the region is very sparsely settled, and the blacks have the reputation of being very wild.'

Now he began explaining in more detail how this affected him. Mrs Lambert had not actually drowned, as I had heard from the Reeds, but had been helped ashore by the three other survivors. She had been unwell during the voyage, and had been left resting on the beach whilst the others climbed a nearby dune in an endeavour to see what lay beyond. They could see a string of large lakes apparently blocking the way inland, and had decided to walk along the beach to Port Albert, fifty miles to the west. However, when they returned to where they had left Mrs Lambert, she had disappeared. Her footprints had led them behind the first line of low dunes, but the wind was blowing briskly, and the sand had filled in the tracks beyond that. They had looked and called for a while, but seeing smoke from aboriginal' camp fires, and being unarmed, they had been too frightened to go further.

'I can't blame them,' said Mr Lambert in a bitter voice, 'but my poor wife could not have been far away. She was sick and exhausted. She must have been perhaps within earshot. Now, three weeks ago, I received some disturbing news from Melbourne. There are rumours current that a white woman is living with the blacks near the Gipps Land Lakes. Oh, it is all very vague and conflicting. Some say it is impossible. Others say that the region is so wild that the blacks could easily hold a white person hostage without being found, even though much of the land is held under lease by squatters. The blacks have the advantage. They can move about country which is impassable to a white man. For the past week, I've been preparing to go myself to Gipps Land and get to the bottom of this story.'

His light brown eyes fixed on me, penetratingly.

'And you, Miss Smith, are going to help me.'

'But how can I help you?' I protested, sure that I was in the clutches of a madman.

'As things stand, Miss Smith, I'm reasonably

sure that my poor wife is dead. I gave up hope some time ago, and my children are learning to accept that they'll never see their mother again. But now, Miss Smith, whatever happens, I shall bring a white woman back from Gipps Land.'

Now I began to understand what all this was about. Foxy Lambert had a shady scheme in mind, and intended that I should be his accomplice. I decided to hear him out.

'I had no idea of such a thing until half an hour ago. But, Miss Smith, you rather resemble my poor Elizabeth. Oh, you're fair, and she was dark, but there is a similarity in the shape of your face and the colour of your eyes. You are fairly like her in build, enough for my purpose.'

Amazed though I was, I still recollected that Mrs Chisholm had mentioned my likeness to someone she knew, and I knew that this person must have been Mrs Lambert.

'I — I won't be a party to any swindle,' I said.

He laughed, without mirth, but with a knowledge of all that was on the seamier underside of human existence.

'Miss Smith, let's understand one another. You're running scared. I sensed it the moment you entered this room. You're no little servant girl who's stolen two shillings. You're in desperate trouble. I don't want to hear what it is. That'll only make me your confederate. And I'm planning a swindle. My father-in-law died recently. He left a very strange will. My late wife's part of the estate does not come to me, as it should have. It reverts to his widow.'

The late Mr Eldridge had understood his son-in-law, I thought.

'And you want me to impersonate your wife so that you can inherit her share,' I said, very slowly, chewing on each word.

'You're intelligent,' he said, approvingly.

'And what will happen to me when you've — you've managed this fraud?'

'You'll go on your way a hundred pounds richer. To the arms of your fiancé, if there is such a person.'

'And how soon shall we leave?' I was turning all this over in my mind with frantic speed.

'We'll leave for Melbourne on the tide tomorrow afternoon. Never fear, Miss Smith, I'll keep you out of sight.'

In Melbourne, I thought with the confidence born of two occasions upon which I had successfully managed to show a clean pair of heels, I shall give you the slip. I don't

94

want your hundred pounds. I don't want your shady schemes. But I do want to take myself as far from Sydney, and the long reach of the Furlongs, as possible. Jim is only twenty miles out of Melbourne. He loves me. He'll help me.

And what was the alternative? As if it had happened but five minutes before, I could hear Mrs Furlong screaming her accusations at me.

'All right,' I said.

It was dangerous, and it was hare-brained, but I had already learnt that, alas, for many of us, the only way to keep one's head above the stormy waters of life is to grab whatever opportunity floats by. At the same time, I seemed to see the lovely eyes and saintly features of Mrs Chisholm reproaching me. After such a good and virtuous start in New South Wales, I was now plunging recklessly into a nefarious adventure.

I took a very deep breath.

'All right,' I said. 'I'll do what you want.'

'Good.' Mr Lambert took out a large gold timepiece and consulted it. 'There's no time to lose. I'll find you some better clothes than those, and instal you in safe lodgings.'

Mr Lambert, I learnt very quickly, was a man of action. The first thing he did was work out my new identity. I was a boy, he declared firmly, not a young man. By fixing my age at about fourteen, many problems would be avoided. I was his nephew now, newly arrived from the Old Dart, to be trained into colonial ways by his successful uncle. My name — and it was his observation, founded no doubt upon his own criminal career, that aliases were easier to remember if the initials remained unchanged — became Christopher Shaw. Young Kit was then suitably outfitted in new readymade clothes which Mr Lambert bought after measuring me up with a piece of string. (For obvious reasons, he did not dare take me into a store.)

He offered no explanation as to why I had to be a boy when eventually I was to be his wife, and the lodgings he chose for me added to my growing unease. They consisted of a small room in an inn of the lower type, situated in the infamous Rocks area, haunt of ex-convicts, prostitutes and common seamen. The landlord was an old friend of Mr Lambert's, judging by the intimate nature of the conversation they held just out of my hearing.

Mr Lambert came into the bedroom with me, shutting the door behind him with a decisive slam, and I saw, to my surprise, that he held a large pair of scissors and a comb in one hand.

'I'm going to trim your hair,' he announced.

'No,' I said, more to show that I still possessed some independence than for any other reason.

'Yes, Miss Smith. You can trust me. At one stage in my career, I was personal servant to a military gentleman. If I hadn't made a good job of trimming his hair, he'd have had me tied to the flogging tree for fifty of the best.'

When he had trimmed my shorn hair to his satisfaction, he announced that he would leave me alone for a few minutes while I changed into my new clothes. As soon as he had gone out, I looked at myself in a scrap of looking glass which hung on the wall, and was agreeably surprised at the reflection therein. Mr Lambert had trimmed my hair in a way which was quite becoming and yet, undeniably boyish.

Duly, he inspected me in my new clothes, and frowned, not quite satisfied.

'Don't strut like that,' he rebuked me. 'You look like an actress playing a man's part.'

'Well, I am,' I replied.

'Miss Smith, there is no need to be impertinent. You need me probably far more than I need you. Now, Sam'll bring you a meal himself. You can trust him. He owes me favours from the old days. But afterwards, bolt your door.'

There were bugs in the bed, and unsettling noises from outside. I lay there until after midnight, scared and lonely, before I fell asleep. Then it was to dream, of the things I had tried so hard to forget, and which could not be forgotten. My father lying dead with Antoinette beside him, and my grandfather crumpled upon the stairs, with Mrs Furlong, who wore the face of the old fortuneteller, accusing me.

'*Lost! Lost! Lost!*'

I was awake, and it was dawn, and I began to sob, helplessly, into that grubby pillow.

8

Mr Lambert escorted me on board the *Kerry Lass*, the craft upon which I had intended to stow away, and, after the briefest of exchanges with the master, I was shown into a very small cabin.

There were two bunks, and hardly enough room otherwise to move, but I immediately noticed a quantity of luggage therein.

'Do I have to share this with someone?' I asked, taken aback.

'That is my luggage, and this is my ship, Miss Smith.' Then he softened slightly. 'Stop worrying. I'm shipping five horses aboard, and I intend watching them during the nights. I'll sleep during the day. Now, Miss Smith,' he continued, 'I have to go ashore for some hours. If you try to run away, I'll have you dragged back and charged with stealing a new set of clothes.'

'If you do that, I'll tell the magistrate about your plan.'

'And who'd believe such a thing of me?' The laugh was more hateful than ever. 'I'm very rich, and known to be thoroughly reformed. Who'd take your word against mine?'

No wonder, I thought, sitting on the edge of the lower bunk and staring grimly out of the minute porthole at water reflecting the grey of cloudy skies, there are so many stories about the cunning ways of foxes. No wonder it needs a horde of dogs and horses and men to catch one.

Mr Lambert arrived back mere minutes before we sailed, and I saw him saying farewell to two little girls who were then led back to a carriage by a dour, thoroughly respectable-looking woman who must have been the nursery governess. What a hypocrite you are, I thought, but we'll see who is the smarter one when we reach Melbourne.

When we left the shelter of the harbour and struck the great swells of the Pacific, I was glad to snuggle into my sea jacket, and with my new knitted cap pulled well down past my ears, watched the coastline recede as we headed for open water. After that long, dreary voyage from Britain, I had not wished to go to sea again, but, unexpectedly, I enjoyed the feel of spray against my cheek and the sounds about me as the sails creaked and strained. Now that I had left Sydney behind me, I felt safe and elated, and thought forward happily to my reunion with Jem.

My new buoyancy of spirit was enhanced

by discovering, very soon after leaving Sydney Heads behind us, that Mr Lambert was a poor sailor. That he was not as infallible as he had appeared at first was definitely an omen favourable to my chances of escape.

'Takes Mr Lambert a day to get his sea legs,' the master informed me, as I ate with him and the mate in the cuddy. 'You're a lucky young fellow to have a successful man like him taking you under his wing,' he added, and I nodded silently in reply.

They must have thought that I was an odd, silent recluse of a youth, but I did not trust my ability to keep my voice down to a suitable pitch for anything more than the briefest remarks.

Mr Lambert had recovered by the following afternoon, and apart from telling me to watch my tendency to walk in a female way, and one or two other remarks of a similarly critical nature, he had little to say to me. As he had promised, he slept during the day, in the lower bunk, and kept watch over the horses during the night.

In the day time, I discovered, the horses were cared for by a villainous looking pair, an elderly man with 'old lag' written all over his seamy face and the habit of chewing tobacco, and a plump Maori with a tattooed chin and cheeks. The former was Isaac Purtle, and the latter, with an unpronouncable name of at least six syllables and nineteen letters, was called Maori Mick, Mick for short.

This amount of solicitude for horses was not unusual in New South Wales, where even sheep were ahead of humans as subjects for conversation. Mr Lambert intended taking these animals on his search for Mrs Lambert, and their fitness was of prime importance.

Now, as our little ship nosed westwards into the Bass Straits, with a sinister reputation built upon many shipwrecks and the viciousness of sealers living by their own laws, I had no thought of tragedy. Settled in my bunk for the night, I was quite optimistic. There was no doubt that I would reach Melbourne before any message from the Reeds, and once I found out where Jem was living, I would walk there if necessary. I was a stranger to Melbourne, but then, from what I had picked up at mealtime conversations, so was Mr Lambert, which could only make my escape easier. It was imperative that I spoke to Jem before he discovered from other sources that I had been deceiving him. I still had no very clear idea of what we would do when he learned that I was not Miss Starling, but Miss Furlong (alias Miss Smith) and that a warrant for my arrest had arrived from Britain. Perhaps we could go to the Swan

River settlement in the far west of Australia, or to New Zealand, or even to the Cape Province in Africa.

'Miss Smith,' said Mr Lambert's voice in my ear, with all that sudden loudness of a sound which arouses one from deep sleep, 'you'd better be up and dressed. We have to be ashore with the horses before the tide turns.'

I raised myself slightly, and Mr Lambert, who had hoisted himself up to awaken me, jumped back to the floor of the cabin.

'We're not in Melbourne already!' I exclaimed, quite incredulous. Last night, we had been off the Ninety Mile Beach, with the great southward jutting peninsula of Wilson's Promontory between us and Port Phillip Bay upon the shores of which stood Melbourne.

'No,' replied Mr Lambert, picking up his odds and ends of luggage and thrusting them into one large canvas bag. 'We're almost at Port Albert.'

'But I thought we were going to Melbourne!' My dismay must have been revealed in my voice, because he looked up at me sharply.

'Why on earth should we go all the way to Melbourne and then come back to Port Albert?' he demanded. 'Come on, hurry up. If Captain Mills doesn't catch this tide, he'll be stuck here until tomorrow. It's dangerous to leave by night.'

So saying, he picked up his bag and left me to ponder this latest development. All along, I had assumed that we would go to Melbourne first, there to put together an expedition. For a few minutes, I debated with myself whether to refuse flatly to disembark here at Port Albert, but I knew too well that I needed Mr Lambert's protection until the right moment came for my escape.

When I went out on deck, dressed and with my few odds and ends packed, I could see easily why the master was in a hurry to deposit his passengers and leave. Although we were now in calm waters, scattered about were a number of low, sandy islands, forming a natural barrier against the fierce gales of the Straits, but at the same time providing only narrow and dangerous channels for incoming and outgoing vessels. As I stood watching the flat green land approach, Mr Lambert fairly pounced on me.

'Come on,' he said, 'we need your help.' Then: 'You can't wear your hat like that! For heavens' sake, remember you're supposed to be a boy.'

So saying, he grabbed both sides of the brim of that wide-brimmed hat I had arranged carefully at a flattering angle, pulling them down over my ears. I was sure that I must now appear half-witted, but he was satisfied.

'That's better,' he muttered. 'Now come and help us. A strong healthy boy like you shouldn't be standing there watching us work.'

'I'm sick of being a boy,' I whispered, biting back my fury. 'I'll tell the captain I want to go on to Melbourne.'

'Well, you're not going to.' He had taken my arm, and he gave it a hard pinch. 'I need you here. And you need me, nephew, remember?'

This was unanswerable logic, and I grudgingly assisted in the work of moving our goods ashore, hating Mr Lambert more by the second.

For such a small expedition, there was a huge amount of gear. There were saddles and harness for the horses, and saddlebags and pots and cups and blankets and other necessities like hatchets and rope and pieces of canvas. As we watched the *Kerry Lass* heading out to open sea, I wanted nothing so much as to fall on to the soft sand of the beach and rest. All my life, I had envied the freedom accorded menfolk, but after only a few days, I wanted ardently to be restored to my own sex.

'Come on,' snapped Mr Lambert, as Maori Mick and Isaac Purtle urged the horses forward, 'and keep that hat down over your face. I don't want anyone in Port Albert to remember your features too well.'

'Why?' I asked, still determined to needle him.

'Because, when we return, you'll be a woman, and people aren't so stupid that they won't notice a resemblance. I want you to stay here with Mick and Isaac, and don't open your mouth more than necessary.'

At least, his insistence on keeping me dressed as a boy had been explained. It was the easiest way to smuggle me past Port Albert into the wilderness, so that he could produce his 'wife' after a pretence at searching for her.

As for Port Albert, what a miserable little place that was! Beyond the cleared land of the township — appearances notwithstanding, Port Albert had been duly declared a township, with town lots up for sale — the bush stood solidly, as if quietly waiting for the chance to snatch back the few acres which had been taken. The land about was flat, with hills purple to the north, all hung about with a great air of emptiness. Although it boasted the title 'Port', there was no wharf, only a little jetty before a sorry cluster of huts. Cattle lowed in crudely fenced yards, awaiting shipment across the Straits in a small coastal vessel which lay at anchor.

Yet, after those first lean months during which the founders of Port Albert had almost starved, and had been in constant peril from the blacks, whom they scared off with shot from an old cannon, the place was now well established. Cattle were shipped several times a month across to Van Diemen's Land which, being mountainous, had little space for the broad pastures needed to raise beef.

As if to mock the fact that my plans had gone awry, I could hear, with increasing faintness, one of the crew of the *Kerry Lass* calling out soundings as the vessel vanished beyond the islands. Mr Lambert strode off towards what seemed to be the main buildings of Port Albert, after telling us, sternly, to stay with the horses. It was hard to guess why people had chosen to come here, and what hopes and failures had driven them to attempt a new life in this isolated place. But they had come, and were somehow making their lives here. There was washing on a clothes-line or two, smoke coming from chimneys, vegetable gardens in the making, and a child making mud pies in the middle of the main street. There were also three stockmen in Highlanders' bonnets celebrating their arrival in civilisation from somewhere beyond and, as they were quite drunk at nine o'clock in the morning, they had probably started their drinking the previous day.

Isaac Purtle looked towards them, enviously.

'Lor', I've an awful thirst,' he said.

'Mr Lambert wouldn't like it,' I said, grabbing a little bit of authority.

Isaac Purtle looked taken aback, but he settled down to saddling up the horses.

'The 'orses should 'ave a spell before we go orf into the bush,' he grumbled. 'But Mr Lambert's got this bee in 'is bonnet that we should git goin' quick as possible.'

'He knows you get thirsty,' said Maori Mick in a surprisingly soft voice.

'Now, none o' your lip, you 'ymn-singing savage,' retorted Isaac Purtle.

Maori Mick did not take umbrage, but grinned to himself.

Mr Lambert came back after about ten minutes, telling Maori Mick to accompany him to the store, to pick up provisions for the journey. He had something else to say. Another expedition seeking the lost white woman had arrived in Port Albert two days since, and had departed the previous afternoon for the lakes region to the north east.

'They've a dray and a whaleboat,' he added, 'and are travelling along McMillan's track. We should be able to get ahead of them without much bother.'

Now he really was in a hurry, and it was barely noon when our little caravan, four persons on horseback and one pack horse, moved along Port Albert's only street towards its companion village, Tarraville, which was not much more than a stone's throw distant. Why there should have been two townships when one would have sufficed, I do not know, but other settlers had arranged themselves near the bank of a pretty little stream called the Tarra, after Charlie Tarra, aboriginal guide who had led Count Strezlecki through the ranges which now bear the Pole's name.

'I hope you can manage astride,' said Mr Lambert to me, as if thinking of this for the first time.

'I used to ride a donkey when I was a child,' I said, which surprised him, but, as I soon found out, this and the one hour I had spent riding that horse upon which I had fled from the Reeds' farms was hardly preparation for our expedition. Still, I managed well enough, aided by pride and a stubborn determination not to look a fool. Mr Lambert kept close to me, and enlarged upon what he had learnt from the people of Port Albert.

The whole of eastern Gipps Land, it seemed, was buzzing with rumours about the captive white woman. He explained that he had been told by the storekeeper back at Port Albert that the first clue had come to light right there in the estuary of the Albert River, no distance at all from his store, when a canoe captured from hostile blacks had been found to contain part of a woman's dress and an article of underwear. Local blacks had said that a white woman was living with the blacks whose territory lay about the lakes forty or so miles away.

The storekeeper believed the story, because, he said, other scraps of information were to hand. Men exploring the shores of the lakes for Mr McMillan mentioned that they had seen a European-looking person at one camp, and someone else had found initials carved into a tree near Bruthen Creek. However, another man who was in the store at the time scoffed at the story. The clothing had most likely been stolen off a clothes-line.

Perhaps, the storekeeper had said; but there were hardly any women in Gipps Land, white women that is, and if clothes had been stolen hereabouts, he'd have heard of it. (Such is the stuff news is made of in out-of-the-way places like these.)

'The other party cannot be far ahead of us,' continued Mr Lambert. 'They left in the middle of the afternoon yesterday, and got themselves bogged before they'd gone two miles. They made a bit of a mystery about what they intend to do, but they've a boat with them, so obviously they intend to sail about on the lakes. Now, I'd intended that we'd follow McMillan's track all the way to a village called Flooding Creek, which is about thirty miles from the place where the ship was wrecked, and hire a black guide. But I don't want to be mixed up with this other expedition. So we're going to leave the track and push across country as best we can. I've a map and a compass, and provided we don't go far inland and keep the coast on our right, we shouldn't get ourselves lost.'

I did not much like this idea. Since my arrival in New South Wales I had heard innumerable stories of men disappearing in the wilderness, and skeletons, identified as European, being found in remote gullies where the poor owners had perished from lack of food and water.

'The last thing I want,' announced Mr Lambert, 'is for our rivals to see you. As soon as we're past Tarraville, we'll leave the track.'

Tarraville was very much like Port Albert, except that it had no harbour, and only two men drinking from bottles outside the public house instead of three. Once again, Isaac Purtle remarked that he was thirsty, and Mr Lambert, deliberately misunderstanding him, said that we would stop and boil up a pot of tea after another mile or so. A man spading over dirt in a yard, overcome by curiosity at seeing so many strangers in one day, told us that 'Mr LeFevre's lot' were about three miles along the track. One of the drays had been bogged again.

Away from the track, the country was almost at once much wilder and less open. On the credit side, the bush here was of a greenness quite unknown near Sydney and, it being spring, the wattles were a-bloom in all their varieties ranging from nasty prickly shrubs to tall trees splashed with gold. Unhappily, all this lushness sheltered swarms of mosquitoes which, for sheer ferocity and persistence made their Sydney cousins seem poor things indeed. Once or twice, I saw swallows weaving and diving as they gorged on the insects which arose in such swarms from the pools and undergrowth; but however replete these energetic and pretty little birds — their necks were collared with a band of rusty red feathers — were by the time they settled for the night in a hollow tree, their efforts made no difference to the numbers of those nuisances.

Now Mr Lambert gave the signal to dismount, and in a small clearing from which two kangaroos had moved off as we arrived, the three men held a council of war.

'Do y' reckon we'd be best goin' along the beach?' suggested Isaac Purtle, screwing up his pouched eyes against the sun.

'No. Too exposed, and we might have trouble finding fresh water.' Mr Lambert had crouched down and spread out his map on the ground, and the other two men bent over to follow his finger as it traced our intended route. He was smoking one of his abominable cigars, which is probably why he was untroubled by the mosquitoes.

No one had asked my opinion about what we should do. More than anything, I wanted to return to Port Albert, board that grubby little tub which was taking on a load of cattle, and sail back to civilisation immediately, there to cope with my problems in comparative comfort. Looking back, the major irony of my existence is that I had never longed for adventure but, instead, had always yearned for a settled, secure existence.

9

'This fellow, LeFevre,' said Mr Lambert, 'will follow McMillan's track, of course.'

I edged around, and leaning over, studied the map across his shoulder. McMillan's track went roughly northeast from Port Albert, skirting the main part of the ranges we could see inland, and crossed them at a place called, quaintly, Tom's Cap. He began explaining to his two henchmen — what else could one call these two evil-looking persons? — and as I had heard it all before, I looked about the clearing without much interest. To one side, acting as a natural windbreak, was a thick stand of paperbarks, a tree in the habit of growing very closely and, as I turned slightly, I saw something out of the corner of my eye, beyond a huge old gum tree. Was it a tall 'old man' kangaroo?

It was no use trying to reassure myself. It had been a blackfellow, naked except for the skin rug flung about his shoulders. Nervously, I looked again, and saw nothing except a pair of black and grey birds flying from one tree to another.

Then, like an echo, there was a cry

from somewhere in the forest which grew away from the edges of this bracken-clothed clearing. The horses made restless sounds, and two birds, unidentified, clacked angrily at one another in the high branches. There was no other indication of life, and when the birds had concluded their exchange, no sound save a whispering of the breeze through leaves.

'Dark people,' said Isaac Purtle. 'Don't seem as though they want to show theirselves.'

'I think I saw a black,' I volunteered. 'He had a fur rug over his shoulders, and I thought it was a kangaroo.'

'If it didn't 'op it were human,' commented Isaac Purtle, and spat out a long stream of tobacco juice. 'We'd best mount up, Mr Lambert. Safer on 'orseback.'

Mr Lambert looked towards me, and for a moment, he frowned, and bit at his lower lip, as if trying to make up his mind. For a few seconds, at least, he was concerned about my safety, but after a brief indecision, he told us to get ourselves up on the horses. The blacks were most likely a small party from the northeastern mountains, out of their own tribal lands, and if they had been going to attack us, they would have done it a few minutes before, when we were most vulnerable. The local tribes-people, he had been told at Port Albert, were quite friendly (or cowed), and if the man I had seen had been one of them, he would have come forward to speak with us.

So we formed ourselves into our little cavalcade once more, but this time, I was placed protectively in the middle, for I alone carried no firearms. Yet, we were not in unexplored country, for from time to time, we heard cattle lowing, and once we crossed a set of wheeltracks, left by a settler's dray. Later, on a low hill, we all drew rein, and looked back towards Tarraville. Across the thickly packed treetops, we could see stretches of sea, and the hummocky islets which formed a chain towards the bulk of Wilson's Promontory, mountainous and purple in the distance.

'We'll go a little further, and camp for the night,' announced Mr Lambert, turning his horse, decisively, away from this panorama.

Shortly afterwards, we crossed a small creek, and Mr Lambert decided that this place, with fresh water close at hand, would do for our first night's camp. Now that the sun was low behind the trees, there was a chill in the air, more like that I remembered from my stay in England than any I had experienced since coming to New South Wales, and I thought wistfully of my snug bunk aboard the *Kerry Lass*. Not only was I cold, but sore in every joint and muscle. My hours in the saddle had left aches in parts of my body of which I had hardly been aware until now, and it was in a state of miserable sulks that I huddled down by the campfire to sip at black tea brewed in a quart pot. I did not like the flavour overmuch, but at least it was hot, and warmed me a little. Mr Lambert, who, in his smart riding clothes, seemed more like a city gentleman out for a recreational ride than a bushman, was taking all these discomforts in his stride, quite as well as the Maori and Isaac Purtle.

'Funny thing,' remarked Isaac Purtle, a little later, 'but I reckons there's a sheep over yonder.'

'Plenty sheep about,' said Maori Mick, in between puffing on his clay pipe, and slapping at a mosquito as he spoke. I felt an unexpected kinship with the Maori. Like myself, he was a tyro on horseback and, judging by his groans and complaints, as sore as I was. This made me wonder all the more why someone as clever as Mr Lambert had chosen someone so unsuitable for his expedition.

'Should be folded by sunset,' pointed out Isaac Purtle, confident in his knowledge.

'The shepherd's probably too drunk or

too lazy to care,' commented Mr Lambert, smothering a yawn. 'Miss Smith had better settle down and try to sleep. We'll keep watch in turns, in case our dark friends have it in their heads to steal what they can.'

Mr Lambert's two confederates had been told that I was a woman earlier in the day, and seemed to take it as a matter of course. From long experience, I thought bitterly, they have ceased to be surprised at whatever he does.

Despite the cold, the hard ground, and the ever-present mosquitoes, I slept fairly well, and awoke at dawn to discover that we were being invaded, not by blacks, but by sheep.

'There must be a hut nearby.' Mr Lambert waved a small branch at the silly, woolly beasts as he spoke. 'I daresay we'll find a few that have been killed by the wild dogs before we go far.'

We did not, but we found the hut twenty minutes ride from our camp, in a clear expanse cut from the open woods through which we now moved. It was fairly typical of the dwellings with which stockmen and shepherds made do, a sorry little box built roughly of split timber, with a scrap of roof extending in front to form a veranda. The chimney was also built of wood, and was no doubt lined with clay inside, but no smoke emerged from its aperture.

Isaac Purtle noticed this too.

'Somethin' wrong, Mr Lambert. There's no smoke comin' from the chimney. 'Is breakfast fire'd still be alight.'

Mr Lambert slid from his saddle, and carefully loaded his two pistols, whilst the others did the same with their guns.

'Don't look,' said Mr Lambert to me.

But I had seen, and try as I could, I was unable to turn my eyes away. Two dogs, their heads smashed in, lay in the cleared space in front of the hut, and the door had been half torn from its leather hinges, while all about the few contents lay wantonly strewn across the muddy earth. The hut-keeper, most of the clothing torn from his body, was face down near the door, his bald skull smashed in and a spear still standing up from his back.

If I could have screamed, there would have been relief, but I was in shock. Other images danced before my eyes, superimposed on that pitiful scene. Instead of that shepherd, I saw my own father, and Antoinette, together on the upstairs landing of the villa back in Naples, and mixed up in it were the old fortune-teller, and Mrs Furlong, accusing me. Maori Mick reached up and pulled me off that horse, and I turned and pushed my face against the animal's side, trying to recover myself.

'They've taken all the blankets. We'll have to use one of ours. But first get that spear out of the poor devil.' Mr Lambert's voice floated to me through the mists which surrounded me, and then was close, as his hand rested on my shoulder. 'I've a little brandy amidst my luggage, Miss Smith. Would you like some?'

I shook my head, still not looking back towards the hut.

'All right. But come and sit on the chopping block. If your horse moves, you'll fall forward on your face.' This, of course, was so very typical of Mr Lambert, who had the knack of reducing everything to flat practicality. It annoyed me, and when he tried to take my arm, I shook it away, and walked across to the chopping block myself, sitting down just before my knees buckled beneath me.

'Must 'a' bin killed late yesterday,' commented Isaac Purtle. 'That's why the sheep weren't folded.'

Now the three of them held a conference. Isaac Purtle thought that they should return to Tarraville and report the murder. Mr Lambert did not want to return to Tarraville. This hut plainly belonged to a station

120

holding, and the main homestead should not be too far distant. He rather fancied it was the one marked on his map as being on the Bruthen Creek, which was just a few miles ahead of us. To him, the problem was whether we should take the body with us, or give it decent burial here.

Maori Mick took no part in the discussion, but as the others talked, he dug energetically with a spade he had found amidst the litter of possessions scattered about. This hole was for the dogs. When they had been neatly covered, he leaned on the spade. It reminded me of my father's favourite play, which he had read aloud to me. You can't read Shakespeare, he used to say, you have to listen to it. I think that is what he missed more than anything else during his years of exile — the English theatre. In my happy days, when tragedy had been the subject of delicious shudders on winter nights when the rain pounded against our windows, and shadows from the fire flickered, I had heard the clownish gravedigger's song with a nice feeling of horror.

A pickax and a spade, a spade,
For and a shrouding sheet:
O, a pit of clay for to be made
For such a guest is meet.

Inexplicably, sitting there on that chopping block by that ransacked hut in the Gipps Land wilderness, I began to shriek with laughter. The shepherd's body now lay decently wrapped in a blanket, awaiting a decision from Mr Lambert as to where it should be buried.

Mr Lambert's open palm struck me with a sharp force across the cheek.

'Stop it, you stupid girl,' he said.

'It's like the grave-yard scene in *Hamlet*,' I gasped, my own hand to my face. My laughing had stopped. As much as anything I was astonished. Whatever else had happened in my life, this was the first time anyone had ever laid a violent hand on me.

'Wherever did you hear about the graveyard scene in *Hamlet*?' he jeered. 'Now, pull yourself together. We're going to bury the poor fellow here, and I want it done decently.'

'I'll never forgive you for hitting me,' I said, adjusting myself back to my surroundings. 'No gentleman would ever do a thing like that.'

'You're not a lady, so what does it matter?'

While this shameful little scene was taking place, with the poor shepherd's body not fifteen feet away, and his murderers perhaps lurking in the very trees which surrounded this crudely cleared paddock with the stumps still sticking up out of the ground here and there, Isaac Purtle and Maori Mick had shown a refinement of feeling somewhat unexpected in two rough men. Isaac had gone into the hut, and Maori Mick was walking about, looking at the ground, selecting a suitable spot for a grave, both studiously ignoring us.

'I got 'is ticket, Mr Lambert.' Isaac came towards us, holding out a scrap of paper. 'Made out in 'Obarton. Plenty o' old 'ands skip across the Straits to Port Phillip and Gipps Land. There's no checkin' on 'em once they gets 'ere.'

Having lived some time in New South Wales, I knew how to interpret this. By 'ticket,' Isaac Purtle meant a ticket-of-leave, or parole, issued to a well-behaved convict so that he could take up employment on his own behalf, but only within the area shown on the parole slip. Many parolees from Van Diemen's Land, if they had the chance, took ship to other parts. A few had settled on off-shore islands, becoming the notorious Straitsmen on the many islands of the Bass Straits, living with Tasmanian or Australian black women they had kidnapped. Others moved as far away as Kangaroo Island off the South Australian coast, working for sealers and whalers.

'I suppose he thought he was free at last,' murmured Mr Lambert, folding up the parole and placing it in his pocket. 'At least, we have a name for him, Arthur Wellesley Pittson. What hopes his poor mother must have had! About the same age as myself. Could have been shipped out the same year.' He spoke so softly that I alone heard him. 'But for the grace of God, there goes Quentin Lambert.' Then he raised his voice. 'Let's get on with it.'

So, with the sun touching noon, Arthur Wellesley Pittson was laid to his rest, with Mr Lambert reciting what sounded like a fairly accurate, if shortened, version of the conventional burial service. Irresistibly, I was drawn back to that other funeral in the tiny Protestant cemetery at Naples, with a travelling English divine sending my agnostic father's soul to rest with the rites of the Anglican church. I had stood there in light rain, numbly, hardly hearing his formal words of compassion as he shook my hand afterwards.

Now, instead of being veiled, I held my widebrimmed hat — a hat like that of my father's murderer — in my hands, in accordance with the conventions that separate men and women as much as their physical differences. There was no need for me to do this. The three others knew that I was a woman, but in my boy's garb it seemed, somehow, more respectful to follow their example and listen to Mr Lambert bareheaded. Ridiculously, I felt tears beneath my lids, silly tears which I had been unable to shed at my own father's funeral, but which sprang forth too readily for an unknown and perhaps bad man who, like William Furlong, had met death violently and suddenly.

Hardly had the last phrases been uttered by Mr Lambert when we all heard hoofbeats and many voices, and, turning as one, we saw a veritable cavalcade approaching us through the scattered trees and scrub. There were two men on horseback, and two bullock teams, one drawing a wagon loaded with supplies, and the other an upturned boat on a flat dray, each of these conveyances having three men in attendance, amongst them two blacks.

Mr Lambert said, 'Amen,' and Maori Mick took up his spade to cover the body with soil, whilst the leading man spurred his horse forward.

'What's happening here?' he demanded, in a most peremptory manner, using the sort of voice which belongs to a man who is always obeyed instantly. I hastily donned my hat, pulling it a little forward, to hide the traces of tears which trembled beneath my lower lashes.

'This poor man was killed by wild blacks yesterday. We have given him a Christian burial.' Mr Lambert paused for a moment, and then, introduced himself briefly. 'We're travelling eastwards,' he added, this being an explanation which did not satisfy the new arrival, judging by the expression on his plump face.

'I'm Edward LeFevre. I'm leading the Melbourne expedition in search of the white woman who is being held captive by those same scoundrelly blacks.'

(I am not quoting Mr LeFevre exactly. He was obviously a well-educated man, but as foul-tongued as the roughest ex-convict navvy.)

If the two aboriginal men who stood not ten yards away understood him, their dark faces, set in those grim and frightening lines characteristic of their race's features when in repose, gave nothing away.

Edward LeFevre now dismounted. He was about twenty eight or nine, I thought, dressed with a certain dash with the ends of a long red silk sash trailing beneath the hem of his jacket, but of an overfed build which accounted for the pinkness of his face on this

126

cool day. Unexpectedly, I caught a grimace from the other horseman, who was dressed in a more practical fashion for the bush.

'Yes. We heard about you at Port Albert. You left the day before we arrived — that is, two days ago. I thought you were on your way to Flooding Creek?'

'We are.' Edward LeFevre's mouth became petulant. 'We were misdirected by a half-witted cowherd. We could see that someone had been before us through the bush, and I decided that this was our chance to be set to rights.'

Once again, out of the corner of my eye, I saw a certain look upon the features of the second horseman, expressing the forbearance of one who has already endured much. At the same time, one of the blacks grinned, transforming his heavy and primitive features into a mask of merriment. I had seen this happen before when something had tickled the funnybone of any one of the blacks who had worked for Mr Reed. Amongst themselves, they were surely the most lighthearted people in the world.

What had really happened was apparent. Mr LeFevre, determined to be right, had misdirected his party. Now, he and Mr Lambert stood and discussed Pittson's murder, while Maori Mick, who had already been busy with hatchet and knife, pushed in a cross at the head of the grave, which Isaac Purtle was overlaying with the few rocks and pebbles he could find in order to discourage the wild dogs. While Mr Lambert was talking, he sent me several looks to tell me to keep out of the newcomers' way, and so I went over to help Isaac Purtle.

'You finish 'ere,' he muttered. 'I wants a word with *them*.'

He nodded towards the two aboriginals, and while I knelt down to my task, Isaac Purtle went over to the two blacks, who were chattering one to the other in their own language. He took out a fig of tobacco, cut it into three, and offered them each a piece, which they accepted promptly. Having thus proved himself friendly, he began talking quietly to them, and the three of them conversed earnestly, with a great deal of sign making and pointing and drawing on the ground with a stick.

'Well, we might as well stop here and eat,' announced LeFevre, glaring at Isaac Purtle as if suspecting that our retainer was inciting his blacks to mutiny. 'You'll join us, Mr Lambert?'

'We've already eaten,' lied the leader of our own expedition, 'and had best be on our way.'

It was six hours since we had eaten, and I was ravenously hungry, but Mr Lambert was in no mood to dally here and run the risk of the others discovering that his nephew was an unrelated young woman bearing a coincidental but convenient likeness to his missing wife. The other party seemed to have settled down for some hours, probably to sort out their own differences and decide what to do next.

The four of us had ridden no more than five hundred yards through the thick scrub when Mr Lambert drew rein.

'Well, Isaac, what did you learn?' he asked.

Isaac grinned.

'The way *they're* goin', they ain't goin' to find nothin',' he said. 'This LeFevre cove has the notion he'll sight the lost woman by sailin' about the lakes. And the dark men back there reckons there's another party out lookin' for her now. Government men, under Captain Dana of the Mounted Police. He's got men from the Melbourne tribe under 'im, and they 'ates the Gipps Land men. Mr Lambert, we could 'a' stopped for a bit back there and 'ad somethin' t'eat.'

'We'll keep going for another mile or so. Captain Dana, eh? I'm starting to believe in this missing white woman myself.' It was not said jokingly, but with a slow thoughtfulness which made me look at him sharply. 'Dana's a very experienced man, I've heard. If anyone can find her, it would be he.'

Now, nursing as I did a considerable resentment against Mr Lambert, I began to think carefully about the dilemma which could face him. Until today, he had never really believed that his wife could be alive, but so much effort was now going into the search that he had to accept the possibility. Therefore, if he tried to pass me off as his missing wife, and she was unexpectedly produced by the other searchers, he would be in a very embarrassing position. There was yet another aspect to the matter, and one which sent a chill of fear down my spine. Mr Lambert had airily outlined his cunning swindle, and I had taken it at its face value. But how did I know for sure that he really wanted his wife to be alive, even if she were found?

If he wished to inherit her share of her father's estate, there was no point in allowing her to live beyond the time required to establish that she had survived her father. If I were to act out the part myself, sooner or later would I be required to die so that Quentin Lambert could add to his fortunes?

10

However frightened I may have felt inside, I kept up an attitude of icy contempt towards Mr Lambert through our delayed meal (abominably cooked by Isaac Purtle) and about five miles of lightly timbered country. This open land, thick and green with spring grass between the scattered trees, was far more suitable for grazing than the coastal scrub which had made our progress so slow and difficult earlier that same day. We had turned inland for two reasons: firstly, to dodge a large and swampy lagoon lying behind the dunes of the Ninety Mile Beach, and secondly, to report Pittson's death at the main station of this huge leasehold run.

We saw small groups of cattle occasionally, which meant that white men were near, and from time to time, we encountered kangaroos and their smaller editions, the squat wallabies. Always there were the cockatoos, white ones sitting in flocks in the upper branches of dead trees, or the black variety, as well as their gorgeous cousins, the parrots, red and green and blue and yellow, with a gleam and a sheen on their feathers which vanishes with death and which is never seen amongst captive birds. This country was an ornithologist's paradise. I lost count of the different birds I saw. Some were tiny tits which seemed no bigger than my thumb as they flew away hastily at our approach, and seconds later, in contrast, we passed a group of emus, higher than a man, which moved off with stately and measured tread.

As we travelled, I pondered on ways of ruining Mr Lambert's wily scheme whilst preserving my own safety. Perhaps, at this station we were approaching, I could write a quick letter to Jem, begging his assistance in my plight, but then, would he receive it in time for it to be of any use?

There was no redcoated postman making his daily round here in Gipps Land.

'Miss Smith,' said Mr Lambert, bringing his horse alongside my own, 'I'm sorry I struck you.'

This was so utterly unexpected that I gaped at him, noticing for the first time that he was sprouting a ginger beard.

'Now,' he continued, realising that I was not going to reply, 'I had to do it. You were intent on having a fine old bout of hysterics, and while we fussed about you, those blacks who killed poor Pittson could have crept up on us and speared us.'

That was the most infuriating thing about Mr Lambert. Even at his worst, he always had logic of a sort to back him up. I held up my chin and maintained my silence.

'You know,' he went on, not at all discouraged, 'you puzzle me. When I first met you, I thought you were a typical Sydney slut, quite without feeling or morals. But you're not. You've had a good education, I think, but you're no pampered miss. And you're sensitive, aren't you? You were crying while I did my best with the funeral service.'

'I don't want to discuss anything with you,' I replied, in a low voice. I preferred Mr Lambert when he was behaving nastily. When he was being pleasant, he undermined my determination to somehow see his evil plans in the dust.

So absorbed was I with all this that I had not noticed the threatening slate-coloured clouds which were advancing from the southwest, behind us. Within a few minutes, it was pouring with rain, and when we had forded one of those insignificant rivulets which in Australia are called creeks, we were all relieved to see buildings close by. As we cowered in our saddles with our backs against the sharp gusts of wind, those rough structures appeared to us as a luxurious refuge.

A man who hailed us from the front door of the largest building surprised me by using the words and pronunciation of a cultivated person, and after he had directed Maori Mick and Isaac Purtle towards the men's quarters, he ushered Mr Lambert and his 'nephew' into the main room, where a large fire blazed under the chimney which took up most of one side wall. We had already divested ourselves of our dripping oilskins, and it was good to take off my riding boots and toast my numbed toes before those flames.

Our host, who was young and seemed desperately glad to see new faces, introduced himself as Mason Nesbitt, he being the younger brother of the man who leased this isolated run. The older Nesbitt was a rich businessman from Sydney-side-of-the-Murray, as they called the regions north of the big river which divided what is now Victoria from the rest of New South Wales in those days.

Mr Lambert told this pleasant young man, who was so out of place in these wild surroundings, about the murder and our encounter with Mr LeFevre's party. Mr Nesbitt's reaction was more that of a learned don than of a typical pioneer. He was apt to produce arguments for both sides which balanced everything out, and resulted in nothing.

He had, explained Mr Nesbitt, tried to keep peace with the blacks, but there was continual friction between them and some of the men he was forced to employ. The trouble was, he said, sipping continuously at the brandy he had produced to ward off the chills which he was positive would overtake us without this precaution, the Gipps Land blacks had had experience of the Bass Straits sealers before the settlers had arrived. The problem had been aggravated by Governor Gipps' rulings about punishment being meted out to whites who killed blacks, for this had made the aboriginals believe that they could steal stock, or anything they fancied, with impunity.

While the two men discussed the difficult business, I kept very quiet, acting out the part of Mr Lambert's youthful nephew who was still sufficiently a child to remain silent as his elders talked. Mr Nesbitt seemed relieved that Mr LeFevre would be passing on the news of the killing to police at Flooding Creek. Many another settler would have taken the law into his own hands, and avenged his fellow white man's death, but poor Mr Nesbitt was too civilised to cope with life on the frontier. When in doubt, he turned to the brandy bottle.

Over the usual poor meal, this time of boiled salt beef, dished up by a slatternly woman who was the partner of one of the men employed on the run, Mr Nesbitt told us about himself. Needless to add, while he was doing this, helped on by some of the two bottles of wine he had been keeping for a special occasion, Mr Lambert kept sending me those warning glances of his so that I would not betray my sex. Actually, Mr Nesbitt was so glad to have company that I doubt whether he would have noticed had I worn two heads.

Poor Mr Nesbitt! What a misfit he was! He had, we learnt, studied for the church, but his elder brother — who held the purse strings — had insisted that he come to Australia, placing him in charge of this Gipps Land run. It was easy to guess that this affable, companionable and intellectual young man was suffering agonies of loneliness. It was not merely the loneliness of isolation, for he employed several men, but the far worse loneliness of a clever and erudite young man condemned to a harsh and often brutish life.

(Over the years, tiny snippets concerning Mr Nesbitt have filtered back to me. Exasperated by his junior's frequent drinking bouts, his brother found another manager, and Mr Nesbitt drifted over to New Zealand to fight as a private soldier in one of the Maori wars. Friends lent him the fare back to Britain, where he claimed a small inheritance and resumed his studies, eventually being ordained.)

After dinner, I nodded in a corner near that roaring fire, while the rain lashed down outside, and the two men smoked Mr Lambert's cigars and drank Mr Nesbitt's brandy. I was sleepy from both my long and difficult day and the two glasses of wine I had drunk at dinner, but not so much so that I was unaware that Mr Lambert was becoming very much less reserved. Now, after a lot of hedging as to the purpose of his journey through Gipps Land, Mr Lambert decided to trust our host, and he told the other about his quest for a missing white woman.

'Ah,' said Mr Nesbitt, wisely, peering across at Mr Lambert as if through a mist. 'The white woman! A lot of Melbourne cackle, but 'tis so persistent there could be a trifle of truth in it. Allow me, my friend, to show you something.'

Mr Nesbitt's housekeeping was simplistic. Instead of cupboards, he had a number of chests which doubled up as seats, and after standing up, he opened the lid of the one upon which he had been perched, and produced, after some rummaging, a large calico handkerchief.

It was no ordinary handkerchief, for it was printed on one side in bold, if smudged, letters, and the message was repeated in two languages, English, and another which I was told was Gaelic.

'There are those who say she — if she exists — was a Highland lassie cast ashore northeast from here, along the Ninety Mile, past the entrance to the lakes,' said Mr Nesbitt. 'The last time Mr Tyers the Lands Commissioner passed this way, he left three of those with me. Now, I know there's no white woman on my run, but he'd had orders from Sydney to distribute those handkerchiefs. I nailed up two to please him — he's a capital fellow — and kept that one as a curiosity. The other two soon disappeared — whether the blacks took them or my men are using them as dusters, I don't know.'

I took the calico square, leaning forward towards the front of the fireplace so that I could read the words thereon. The message was hopeful rather than sensible:

WHITE WOMAN. THERE ARE FOURTEEN ARMED MEN PARTLY WHITE AND PARTLY

BLACK IN SEARCH OF YOU. BE CAUTIOUS AND RUSH TO THEM WHEN YOU SEE THEM NEAR YOU. BE PARTICULARLY ON THE LOOK-OUT EVERY DAWN OR MORNING FOR IT IS THEN THAT THE PARTY ARE IN HOPES OF RESCUING YOU. THE WHITE SETTLEMENT IS TOWARDS THE SETTING SUN.

'If she does exist,' went on Mr Nesbitt, pouring out more brandy for himself and Mr Lambert, who, I regret to say, was somewhat intoxicated by now, 'she'd be in the very wild country to the east of the lakes. Fact is, I don't believe in this castaway woman at all. You've seen how the blacks treat their women, Lambert. A white woman wouldn't last a year.'

'I have to make sure,' said Mr Lambert, stonily. Then he thumped a fist on to the crude table. 'She could be my wife. I have to know whether she's dead or alive.'

'Now, listen.' Mr Nesbitt leaned forward, placatingly, 'I don't think she's white at all. I think she's a light skinned halfcaste. You've heard of George Bass, who discovered the Bass Straits back in 1798? He picked up some convicts off an island in the Straits, and put them ashore somewhere near here. He couldn't take them with him back to Sydney

139

because his craft was only a whaleboat. They were never seen again. Now, there's William Buckley they found living with the Melbourne blacks — he'd been with them for thirty years. Who's to say one of Bass's castaways didn't live with the blacks for several years, and father children?'

Mr Lambert thought about this, but offered no immediate comment. Then, abruptly, he asked whether his nephew, who was almost asleep, could retire. I was offered a tiny lean-to store-room attached to the back of the house, a chamber full of chinks and draughts, and with a smelly tallow lamp and a lumpy straw pallet, I was left to my juvenile slumbers. By straining my ears, I could just hear Mr Lambert explaining away my peculiarities. My mother, I learnt, had kept me far too close to her side, and one object in bringing me on this difficult journey was to harden me and make me more fit to face the realities of the world. In addition, probably as a result of my strange upbringing, I was subject to noisy nightmares and I talked in my sleep.

Thus did my wily 'uncle' put forth believable reasons as to why he did not share my bedchamber. I would have preferred a nightly battle for my honour to being made to appear such a weak-minded fool. If it had not been for the evil way in which I had been misled into thinking that we were sailing straight to Melbourne, I thought, as I tried to shake the pallet free of lumps, I could be with my dearest Jem.

I tried to settle myself in this uncomfortable place, wishing that both Mr Lambert and Mr Nesbitt would also retire. To comfort myself, I thought about James Harkness and our first meeting.

* * *

It had not seemed important at the time, although I had been immediately aware that James Harkness was a very handsome young man. I had just dismissed my little class for the day and was tidying things away, when I became aware that a tall man was standing in the doorway of the schoolroom.

'Oh, I'm sorry,' he said, as I looked up, startled. 'I expected to find Miss Minton here.'

'Miss Minton left two years ago,' I replied, starchily, and he had smiled slowly, his suntanned face creasing in a rueful half apology.

'I *am* out of date,' he replied. 'Well, I won't trouble you any more, Miss . . . '

'Starling,' I supplemented, and began

making a great affair of wiping the blackboard.

'Good afternoon, then, Miss Starling,' he said, quite solemnly, and retreated. I was at the window in an instant, watching him, and praying that he would not turn suddenly and catch me. Miss Minton had been married just prior to my arrival at the Reeds' property, and from what I had heard, she had been a flirt. No doubt, this stranger had dallied with her from time to time. I lost him as he turned past the right wing of the house, and it was with a feeling of regret that I locked up my little domain.

As I shared my evening meal with the Reed children, I heard about my handsome stranger. Mr Harkness, they said, was back. Mr Harkness had been managing father's run out near Bathurst, and now our married overseer and his family would be going across the mountains to take over in his stead. The children were upset by this: the Price offspring were their playmates. The Price family, although decent enough in their own way, were roughhewn folk, and I wondered whether Mrs Reed may have had a hand in this decision to remove them painlessly from her own children's sphere.

So, Mr Harkness was not a passing traveller, but someone of whom I was likely to see a great deal. We met again, frequently but briefly, saying things like 'A nice day, isn't it?' or, 'It looks like rain again,' and every time this occurred, I went away and silently kicked myself for being so tongue-tied. Seized by an intense new emotion, I became aware of my physical shortcomings. I was still too thin, and although my eyes were fine enough, there was something unruly and boyish about my looks. Yet, I was feminine enough in all my impulses. I fiddled with my hair, and bit my lips to make them redder, and pulled my stays in as tight as I could to give myself more of a figure.

Too busy worshipping this fine looking young man, with the dark wavy hair and eyes wrinkled at the corners from living so much in the open, I had given little thought to the basic facts of New South Wales life. Mrs Reed brought me back to earth with a thump. Mr Harkness, despite his responsible position as an overseer and his polite way of speaking, was a common ticket-of-leave man, on the same level as many a drunken scallyway who bragged about being a 'legitimate.' Mrs Reed, who had appointed herself the guardian of my welfare, told me this in such a pointed way that I knew that she had noticed my attempts to make myself more attractive whenever Mr Harkness was likely to be nearby.

The disclosure troubled me, and I remembered the warning we young women emigrants had received about not rushing into marriage in New South Wales. Not that Mr Harkness had given the slightest sign that he had matrimonial designs upon myself, but I had begun taking my daydreams seriously. Being in love was, for me, a wonderful state. It made my whole world bright and new, and gave me the hope that my future could be much better than my past.

11

Our leader was in a glum mood that following morning. The bush was washed and clean and beautiful after the heavy rain, with the sunlight picking up those drops of water which had lingered on blossoms or spider webs, but it was made obvious to myself, Maori Mick and Isaac Purtle that the world lay under a cloud and silence was the best policy.

Mr Nesbitt had pulled himself together sufficiently to crawl from his bed and come outside to say goodbye to us, as the station dogs and everyone who was working nearby proffered their noisy goodbyes. For once, the workers on a sheep and cattle run were more sober than their master.

The open country was soon behind us, and we were surrounded by trees of enormous variety. There were the gums in all their species, the acacias, or wattles, at the height of their spring glory, the sheokes with their delicate greyish needles hanging in semi-transparent curtains about their black branches, and the honeysuckle[1] trees carrying grotesque, hairy cones amidst their big, saw-toothed leaves. Further along, I counted dozens of those equally odd, cypress-like trees called native cherries, or ballarts. Nothing about these is as it seems. They are not cypresses, but a relative of the mistletoe, starting life by nourishing on the root of a neighbouring tree. The cherry is another misnomer — it is a mere thickening of the stem, containing the seed, and its resemblance to our luscious European cherries is fanciful.

This then is the Gipps Land bush I carry in my memory, often beautiful, always strange, and frequently frightening, as one imagined that the briefly fleeting shadows one saw amidst the scrub belonged to the black denizens. To a white traveller in such a place, it must always remain a wonder that the original inhabitants could find any nourishment of a vegetable nature. A white man not carrying his own provisions and without the means to kill game would soon perish. As we rode towards the sun that morning, I longed for my drawing pad even as I feared a flight of spears hurled

---

[1] Banksias

from behind the trees.

Suddenly, a spirit of mischief seized me, and I slowed my horse until Mr Lambert, who was riding gloomily at the rear, drew level. This action, incidentally, showed that I was gaining confidence on horseback. At first, I had been entirely at the beast's mercy, but now I was actually feeling some affection for the horse, which really was quite as amiable as Mr Lambert had promised back at Port Albert.

I remarked that my father had always said, on those mornings when he felt unwell, that time was the great healer. There was a pause of some length.

'When I want to know about your father, I'll ask you.'

It gave me pleasure to see my tormentor so miserable, and I began singing a gay Italian tune, or rather, going la-la la-la, for I had almost forgotten the words. Perhaps it was just as well that Isaac Purtle, who was scouting the way ahead, turned and called out to Mr Lambert at that moment.

'There's water through the trees on our right. I reckons it's the narrow lake you told 'us to watch for. If you listens, you can 'ear the sea on t'other side.'

Mr Lambert dismounted, tossing me the reins of his horse as he did so, to put me back into my subservient position. He pushed off through the very dense undergrowth towards the glint of water which could be seen in the near distance, and Isaac Purtle smirked at me.

'Like to 'ave changed places with Mr Lambert last night, miss,' he said. 'Me thirst's bin awful.'

I assumed a lofty expression and did not deign to reply. I had no liking for Mr Lambert, but I knew better than to gossip with the servants. At the same time, the friendly way in which Isaac spoke made me think that I should cultivate him as the ally I might desperately need.

Ten minutes later, Mr Lambert returned.

'We'll boil up some tea,' he announced, curtly. 'We've reached the long lake, as you said, Isaac. The surf's no more than a mile away. I could hear it.'

So, we drank black tea from the quart pot, while our leader pored over the map he had spread out on the ground.

'According to Nesbitt,' he said, after a while, 'we should be able to cross about halfway along this lake. It's dry part of the time at that point, and the water is never more than a few inches deep.'

I murmured to nothing in particular that I was surprised that anyone could remember anything Mr Nesbitt had said.

'Look,' roared Mr Lambert, forgetting all the things which ailed him, 'will you please stop acting so confoundedly *womanlike*?'

Chuckles escaping from the others stopped as he glared at them.

'Now, we've settled that,' he said, 'let's get down to brass tacks. If we continue the way we're going, we'll find ourselves on this peninsula with the narrow lake on one side and Lake Victoria — here — on the other. If we press on, we should be able to camp for the night near our crossing place. Then it's a matter of finding a way to the beach through the dunes on the other side.'

It sounded easy enough, but the way was almost ceaselessly difficult. If we moved too far to the right, we found ourselves in peril of becoming bogged in the morasses which bordered the narrow lake, and if to the left, we would miss the peninsula. We saw no blacks, although we passed a group of abandoned windbreaks once, these *mia-mias* being the only shelter the savages ever built. Isaac Purtle observed that he thought they were keeping an eye on us: perhaps they were frightened that we were seeking revenge for Pittson's murder.

We drew rein on a low hillock about three in the afternoon, and from hence we could see stretches of water through the apparently endless trees, the most westerly portions of the great lake system which drained Gipps Land. Beyond that, far inland, and dark blue in the afternoon sun, were the ranges of the Divide, part of that same great chain of mountains which, near Sydney were called The Blue Mountains.

'I reckons,' said Isaac Purtle, 'we should head inland for Floodin' Creek and get a native guide.'

'That's your thirst, not your sense talking,' said Mr Lambert. 'We can't waste the time. If one of these other parties find a white woman, or a halfcaste, or an albino aboriginal woman, before we've completed our own mission, we're wasting our time. We can't be more than twenty miles from the spot now.'

He sat there, brooding for a few moments, his cigar jutting out from a face becoming increasingly shielded by his growing beard. I thought he looked every bit as disreputable as the other two men.

'Look, Mr Lambert,' said Isaac Purtle then, as if trying to persuade his employer to see reason, 'I don't like it. I don't like it at all. Now there's blacks about. I seen the signs. Bits o' dirt the women's stirred up with their diggin' sticks, a bit o' their food they dropped in their hurry to hide.'

With a new respect, I looked at Isaac Purtle. I had seen nought but the trees and the birds.

'Either they're goin' to kill us, or they're scared. Neither ways I don't like it.'

'If they're as scared as all that, we've no worries. Come on,' said Mr Lambert, sticking his heels into his horse.

Beneath our steeds' hooves, the soil had become white and sandy. There had been a fire through here the previous summer, and although bunches of green had sprouted from the blackened trunks, and the bracken pushed up voraciously through ground still littered with char, it was a depressing place, Isaac Purtle, however, stated that he preferred it to the country we had left. There wasn't much anywhere for a black buck with mischief on his mind to hide, he declared.

'And nothing for the horses to eat,' snapped Mr Lambert over his shoulder.

I began to cultivate Isaac Purtle. Mr Lambert was ahead, and the Maori some yards behind, struggling with the pack horse as well as his own mount. He was no horseman, but he and Isaac took it in turns to manage the pack horse.

'You know a lot about the blacks,' I said, smiling at him winningly.

'Yes, miss,' he replied, suddenly stolid, as

if suspecting my motives.

'You must have lived in New South Wales for a long time,' I went on, persuasively.

'Since I come out with me regiment, miss.'

'You were a soldier?' I was surprised, for I had classified him as a convict right from the beginning. Now I knew that I should have taken more notice of the professional way in which he rode and handled the horses. Isaac Purtle may have been plagued by his unassuaged thirst, but he was a man who knew his job.

'Yes, miss.' He unbent, happy to do a little bragging. 'Served under the Iron Duke hisself, I did, all the way, miss. 'Oped to go to India and see more action after we beat Boney, but they sent me out 'ere. Well, I sort o' settled 'ere.' He began expanding to his new audience. 'Used to go out 'untin' bushrangers. That's why they call them mounted police the troopers, miss. Us real soldiers were the first troopers. Then I did a spell with the government surveyors. They'd have blacks along to be guides, and I weren't too proud to talk to 'em. More sense in a o' lot o' black 'eads than some white men's, miss. Some of 'em's proper rogues, but so's a lot o' our own kind. I kin usually talk to 'em and git sense out of 'em.'

'But you've left the army now, haven't you?'

'Yes, miss. I've worked for Mr Lambert these five years. Look after 'is 'orses. 'E's got a property down Camden way, south o' Sydney, and I'm there most times.'

This was all very strange. In Italy, I had seen very old paintings which lacked perspective. Every detail had been executed with precise detail, but the pictures had quite lacked reality and had appeared out of balance to our modern eyes. From my own experiences with pen and brush I knew how important it was to have every item in its correct perspective.

Now, after this talk with Isaac Purtle, my picture of this whole mysterious enterprise had become lopsided. Before this, my landscape had been dominated by three villainous figures setting about their nefarious business without scruple, with myself dragged along as an unwilling accomplice. But nothing in what Isaac Purtle had told me suggested that he was, or ever had been, a criminal.

'The country's improving,' Mr Lambert called out over his shoulder. 'We'll look for a place to camp for the night.'

We had passed the burnt-out bush, and beneath the horses' hooves, the soil was still

153

sandy, bleached white, an ancient sea-bed lifted up from the ocean's floor by a primeval cataclysm. Although man would have been hard put to raise a solitary cabbage here, dense woodlands closed in about us again. A spiny ant-eater, that odd creature some settlers called a hedgehog, took fright at our approach, and dug itself straight down into the sand, so that only its spines remained visible, like a close clump of mottled reeds. Above us, a great eagle hovered, and for once, all the other birds were silent. They say that Australian birds have no song: this may be so, but they make up for it by constant conversation. As ever, the mosquitoes were voracious, so that however much one was entranced by the varied hues of the wildflowers which thrived on this sandy soil, one longed to be somewhere else.

We made camp a few yards from the shore of Lake Victoria, on a small, tussocky clearing behind the spindly grey-leaved trees which edged a narrow beach. Isaac Purtle set three small fires in a triangle, so that the smoke would discourage the insects, and my small canvas shelter was erected so that I could rest in some privacy. The men were worried about the blacks, who had kept so carefully out of sight, and Isaac and the

Maori kept watch for the first half of the night, whilst I and Mr Lambert each tried to sleep.

The wind rose slightly, after a wonderful sunset fit to shame Turner's best, and the waves of the lake hissed and splashed against the shore, while, with my head near the ground, I could hear a constant reverberation — the breakers of the southern seas beating against the Ninety Mile Beach which was only a mile away. Once, I heard the eerie and sorrowful calls of a group of black swans flying overhead, and I tried to still the fears which crowded into my mind by thinking about Jem.

12

Mrs Reed's revelation about James Harkness having been transported did little to dim my adoration. On the contrary, it deepened my admiration for a young man who, after a bad start, was building a new and successful life for himself.

It is hard to explain how I felt about falling in love, for my childhood experiences had left me with a certain cynicism about love. I knew love had been in part the reason for my father's disgrace and exile, and eventually, the total cause of his death. Love had placed me into my awkward position in life. At the same time, I knew that love could bring me the security and stability for which I longed. Yet, when it arrived, I had not been actively searching for it. Love had simply walked through the door into my schoolroom.

I pined in vain for some sign that James Harkness found me interesting, until Christmas Eve of that same year. The night was stifling, and I had gone outside for a stroll before retiring, in the hope that the fresh air and mild exercise would induce sleep when I finally crawled in under my mosquito net.

'Good evening,' said a voice in my ear as I walked along the drive, not too far from the house, for sounds coming from the men's quarters that night indicated that they were celebrating the festive season in the usual colonial style. Then: 'I seem to have startled you. It's a habit of mine.'

'No, not at all,' I said. 'I — I was thinking of something.' There was no need to add that I was thinking about *him*.

'You shouldn't be out in the dark on your own,' James Harkness chided me. 'Some of the men are drunk, and well, even a well brought up young lady like yourself must know how some of them behave when they've been drinking.'

This concern filled me with a happy warmth which had nothing to do with the closeness of the night, although one little corner of my mind chuckled at his description of me as well brought up.

'I'm going back to the house,' I said. 'I only came out because it was so hot inside.'

'Different from our Christmases back home, isn't it? But we'll have pudding and all the trimmings just the same as if the snow was three foot deep. We used to put hot pokers into our Christmas drinks at home. Did you ever do that?'

Christmas in the Latin countries was not the great feast of the more northern lands, and my father and his friends usually became extremely melancholy and drunk at Yuletide. It was not the sort of thing I wanted to talk about with James Harkness.

'No,' I whispered.

'Still, I expect it was all different at your place. My father was someone's head gardener. We weren't dirt poor, but we weren't exactly gentry, either.'

Jem did not speak like an illiterate peasant, but one could hear the western counties in his voice.

'If we'd been rich, I wouldn't be working here as a governess,' I answered, with a soft laugh.

He took my arm, and stopped walking, so that I had to stop too.

'Do you know what that is up there?' he asked, pointing upwards at a bough overhanging the path. This branch extended from a large old gum tree, the only one near the house, left to provide shade when the land was cleared. Through the narrow, down-hanging leaves I could see the stars and I thought that this is what he meant.

'Which one?' I asked.

'Which — I don't mean the stars. I mean the mistletoe. That thick bunch of leaves

158

just up above us. It isn't like our English mistletoe. It even smells like a gum tree when you crush it. But it's mistletoe of a kind.'

I could feel the warmth from his body as he drew near to me, and when he tipped up my chin, oh so very gently, I was yielding and ready. At first, he merely brushed his lips against mine, making something of a joke of it, but as I responded eagerly, his arms caught me crushingly, and we stood there, locked in mutual passion, until we were both disturbed by the sound of voices from the house. Mr and Mrs Reed were coming outside, complaining about the heat in the house. I was released abruptly.

'They won't like it,' he whispered. 'I'd better go.'

'Couldn't we walk for a while?'

But he merely gave my arm a quick squeeze and hurried away. I wandered indoors in a daze, and went to my room, to lie on my bed in a state of dreamy delight. James Harkness had kissed me, and it was quite as wonderful as my wildest imaginings. I thought too, that I knew now why he had avoided me. He thought I came from a superior class. Perhaps, in a way, he was right, but my mother had been Susan Starling, a farm labourer's daughter. And this was New South

Wales, where a man could be what he chose to be.

So, this was the beginning for me and Jem. After this, we found countless opportunities to meet, and I learnt more about him. He told me that as he had no ties in the Old Country, he intended to stay here in Australia when his time was up at the end of this coming year. To all extents, he had been a free man these past three years, working for wages, and in a position of increasing responsibility.

He was curious about my past, and expressed his surprise that I had become an assisted migrant girl like any ordinary servant or factory girl. I said that I had come upon hard times, and that my parents were dead, which was true as far as it went. He told me that he came from Devon, and I admitted to being born in the North.

'You don't talk like it,' was his comment.

It was hard to explain this away. My particular accent was all my own, compounded of those belonging to my father and his friends, with a small dash of Italian thrown in for good measure. It was no wonder that Jem was puzzled, and because I was frightened that my complicated history would scare him away, I put my arms about his neck, inviting him to kiss me.

Before very long, Jem and I stopped bothering our heads about the past, and began talking of the future. I saw a future of blissful tranquillity spreading out before us when Jem became a free man, able to go where he pleased. He talked of trying to find a piece of land somewhere down in the Port Phillip District, where good country was still available for lease, or of going north to Moreton Bay, and I visualised a snug little wooden house with a garden all about and our bonny children growing up free and strong. I did not long for wealth, only for security and a name which was really mine, and a good man who would protect me from a threatening world. Held close in Jem's arms, as he kissed and caressed me, I felt safe, with a solid barrier between me and the past, which still haunted me in dreams.

The blow fell in March, at the end of a long, dry summer, when the grapes hung ripe and purple upon the vines trained over the trellises near the house, where, on the hottest afternoons, I supervised my pupils in the shade. The first I heard of it was not from Jem, but from Simon Reed, the elder of the Reeds' sons. Like all children, he missed little, and he was most certainly aware of my feelings towards the overseer. Probably, there was also an

161

element of jealousy present. Simon enjoyed being the centre of attention, whether as the moving force in a practical joke, or, more, commendably, for good work done in school time. He liked me. He brought me odds and ends found during his rambles, and asked me the meanings of difficult words he encountered. He frequently dragged me off to show me something which had caught his interest, and as I spent more and more of my spare time with Jem, Simon's six-year-old nose went out of joint.

'Mr Harkness is going to Port Phillip,' he said to me as my little class, numbering seven, galloped out to freedom.

I could not believe my ears. I had seen Jem the previous evening, had in fact crept in by a side door long after the rest of the house was asleep, and he had said nothing about this.

'Oh? I think you're wrong, Simon.'

As I spoke, I tidied away scraps of chalk, and felt my heart thumping uneasily. Simon could be endearing, and he could be obnoxious. He was also sharp-eyed and sharp-eared, and within his childish capacity, usually right.

'I heard Father telling Mother about it,' he said, staring at me in open triumph. 'Mother said it was high time, or you would find yourself in trouble, and they would not be able to replace you in a hurry.'

My cheeks flushed hot. Simon did not know what trouble his mother had meant. I did, which made me angry, but not as angry as Mrs Reed's completely selfish fear of losing a good governess.

'You shouldn't eavesdrop,' I scolded. 'And you should never repeat anything you overhear.'

Jem was away working on another part of the property for the day, and it was not until that evening, as the sun, in the way it did in those latitudes, had dropped suddenly beyond the horizon without the grace of twilight, that I was able to ask him directly.

'Oh, you've heard.'

A fat, full moon, immensely swollen as it emerged from its hiding place in the east, was lifting itself up to give us a little light on this hot night when the insects buzzed and voices carried far through the warm air.

Even in my adoring frame of mine, it did seem to me that Jem perhaps did not sound as distressed as he should have.

'Yes. Simon told me. He heard his parents discussing it.' No need to mention the nastier part of it.

'Will you miss me?' Jem took me in his

arms, loosely, and I pressed my face against his shoulder.

'You know I will.' I replied, wretchedly. 'I'll miss you every minute of the day.'

'Oh, Clytie,' he laughed. 'You'll have some other fellow hanging after you in no time.'

'I won't. I won't.' I was almost in tears as I felt his strength and warmth. I needed his arms about me so very badly. 'Will you come back here?'

'I don't know.' He released me, and linked arms with me as we strolled towards the river. 'My parole ends December. After that, I can pick where I go. But perhaps I'll stay with the Reeds. Mr Reed's brother who's been running the Port Phillip lease is off back to England. That's why I'm being sent down there. He's been poorly. Consumption, they say. If I do well managing the run, Mr Reed might keep me on as manager. That'd suit me for a while, Clytie. It isn't far out of Melbourne, no more'n twenty miles, they say. Melbourne's going ahead, and I'd like to stay and see if it's better for me there.'

My little dreams were crumbling about me. I had known enough of impermanent attachments to be wiser, but who can put sense into the head of a girl in love for the first time?

'Then I'll not see you again?' I was holding

164

back tears so hard that my throat hurt.

'Would it matter?'

My hopes leapt again.

'Yes,' I said simply.

'Clytie, you've never told me that much about yourself, but I've this feeling about you. The first time I saw you, I thought you was a relation of the Reeds. I hardly believed it when I found out you was a bride ship girl. And the way you can draw, and talk about olden times and the Romans and that sort o' thing. I learnt my three R's, Clytie, and I know how to manage a run, but that's all my learning.'

'And I suppose you think because I've read a lot I couldn't keep house,' I blurted out. 'I don't want to be a bluestocking, Jem. Mrs Chisholm decided I'd make a governess and I didn't have any choice.'

I was allowing my tongue to run away with me. As usual, I was jumping in feet first, without looking to find out what was there. The unpalatable truth was that I could not keep house. No doubt, I could learn in time, but no one had ever thought that I should need to know about such mundane things as cooking, home medicine, cleaning, or the thousand and one things required in home management. However, I was sure that all women had an inborn instinct for such things, and that I would soon turn the sorriest bush hovel into a bright and shining home.

'Listen to me, Clytie,' said Jem, and by now the moon was up far enough for me to see every line of his adored face. 'I don't know what this Port Phillip run is like. Mr Andrew Reed had been living very rough, and p'haps that's what's ruined his health. I can't take a girl there. That's what you want, isn't it, to go there with me?'

A little maidenly modesty caught up with me at this point, and I looked away, across the silver mainstream of the river, to the black and grey trees on the opposite bank.

'I couldn't go with you, Jem. You know that.'

'Without getting married, you mean?' he roared with laughter. 'Cunning little minx, aren't you? You've got me thinking you're dying of love for me, but when it comes to the point, you're like all the girls. You're dead set on a wedding ring.'

Now I had lost him. My silly tongue had blundered on, making him think that I was a stupid, husband-hunting chit, instead of someone who loved him so much that she would go through fire itself for him.

Then he sobered.

'And it's not such a bad idea at that,' he

mused. 'If we got on in the world a bit, I'd never have to feel you were letting me down.'

It was hardly the fervent protestation of love for which I longed, and at the same time, this last comment of Jem's did rather show up his ignorance of finer society. I belonged to the artistic rather than to the polite world both by nature and birth. Seated behind a silver teapot, I could easily have turned into a disaster.

'But I'll see what things are like on the Port Phillip run, first,' he added, and kissed me. 'Then I'll send for you, and we'll be wed.'

So we were betrothed, and as I crept to my room much later, I was so happy that I hardly noticed my feet touching the floor.

★ ★ ★

How strange it was that, when thoughts of Jem filled so many of my waking hours, I did not dream about him, except in the most fleeting and frustrating fashion. My dreams were always the same, a re-enactment of that All Hallows Eve, sometimes followed by my father's wife savagely berating me. Or, somehow, events would become mixed up, and both the man in the broad-brimmed hat and Mrs Furlong were pursuing me, as I tried frantically to reach the safety of Jem's arms. That was how he came into my dreams, as a vague and shadowy figure, always a little outside the perimeter of my horrors.

My dreams did not desert me on the shore of Lake Victoria. I could see my father, so hideously wounded, arising and pointing at me, accusingly. 'You have killed me!' he said. 'You have killed me!' I began to run, with the ground sliding away under my feet, so that I made no progress towards my lover, and then, for the first time, miraculously, Jem was there, holding me, so that at last I was safe and secure.

I awoke, and it was a continuation of my dream, for I was being held, tightly, but I could smell cigar smoke, and Jem did not smoke. I was being ardently embraced by Mr Lambert, who had crawled into my tent, and I immediately began pummelling at him with my right fist.

'Miss Smith,' he said, releasing me abruptly, 'you were having a nightmare. I was trying to wake you up. Now, come on. It's time for us to keep watch.'

13

I felt a very great fool as I crept out after Mr Lambert. The two others had already rolled themselves up in their blankets, and Mr Lambert threw more wood on all three small fires before seating himself alongside the spot I had chosen.

'You dream a great deal, don't you?' he asked, quite companionably, lighting a cigar with a burning twig.

Wanting to show him that I disapproved of tobacco, I coughed a few times, and he took the cigar from his mouth, and looked at it.

'Before I left Sydney,' he said mildly, 'I told myself that this was a splendid opportunity to cure myself of the habit. But, alas, somehow, a supply found its way into my saddlebags.' And with this, he thrust it back between his lips.

Of all the things this man had said or done, this seemed to me to be the most hypocritical and extraordinary. While planning a complicated and incredibly hardhearted fraud based on his wife's disappearance, he could at the same time rebuke himself over a comparatively minor failing. So I sat there in aloof silence, still smarting inside over the undignified way in which I had found myself clutching Mr Lambert, for, now that I had sorted it all out, I knew that I was the one who had done the embracing, not he.

It was about midnight, a dark clear night, illuminated only by our fires. Far above, the Milky Way spread out in its entirety across the sky, for this was the time of the equinox, when this mighty congregation of constellations, and the white clouds which have given it its name, is the glory of the southern skies. Those in northern latitudes never see the whole Milky Way, with the Southern Cross moving upwards through its clustered stars before the winter solstice, and then sinking back to its midsummer position above the southern horizon. I remember that my first glimpse of the Southern Cross, during my voyage to Sydney, had been a disappointment. Amidst the stars of the Milky Way it had been hard to find, until I learned to identify the two Pointers, brilliant stars which always lead the eye to the Crux. It is in summer that the Cross is magnificent, as it hangs poised above the Pole.

'Miss Smith,' said my companion then, as I wrapped my blanket about myself, 'would you care to confide in me? You do talk in your sleep, you know, and under the circumstances it's been impossible to avoid hearing you.'

'They say,' I uttered, with an entirely false laugh, 'that I talk a lot of nonsense in my sleep.' Confide in you, I thought. I'd as soon confide in a Borgia!

'That you do. But why should a young woman be so terrified in her dreams?' His voice was so kindly that had it belonged to anyone else, I might have been deceived into thinking that here I had a friend.

'You're not going to tell me, are you?' When he understood from my silence that I had no intention of answering, he spoke again. 'Well, Clytie Smith, it's your own business. Now, tomorrow — or today, rather — I'll have to make up my mind what to do about you. Whether to take you back to Port Albert and send you on your way to Melbourne and then continue my search for this mysterious woman in case she is my poor Elizabeth.'

'Mr Nesbitt thought that the woman is a half-caste,' I suggested, smothering a yawn.

'Mr Nesbitt's point of view is interesting. He's too well-educated to believe every silly yarn going the rounds, but he had invented a logical story to fit the case. That's the whole trouble. It could be true that there is a white woman living with the blacks. I've so many doubts myself now. When you came into my life, Miss Smith, I regarded you as a gift from Providence, a way of pushing my plan through to perfection. How can I explain it? One part of me shrinks at the thought of my sweet, gentle wife being treated as the blacks treat their women. The other part hopes that she is still alive.'

It was strange to hear him speaking thus, for after all, he was a common swindler. But who could really understand Mr Lambert, known to some as Foxy? There is more than one mystery in Gipps Land, I mused, and a fine example is sitting not four feet from me.

I tried to be a little cunning myself.

'I'd like to go back to Port Albert,' I said, 'but I expect then you'd not give me all my money.'

'Ah yes, the money is important.' Mr Lambert sounded amused. 'You'll have your money, the whole hundred pounds, whatever happens. By the way, how are you going to explain away such a large amount to this sweetheart of yours?'

'I'll say that I received a small legacy,' I answered promptly.

Mr Lambert pondered this.

'You did well to come to New South Wales,' he murmured after a few moments.

'You must be very much at home in a country where there are so many sharp wits.'

How could one reply to this? I snuggled down further into my blanket, and began thinking very earnestly of how I could outwit this villain. There was something, I had heard, called turning Queen's evidence, but by going to the law myself, I could well end up on an English gallows platform. It all went round in circles in my head, and the next thing of which I was aware was a strange gobbling noise. I came to consciousness with a frightened start. It was bright daylight, with the lake reflecting the blue skies above. The last thing I remembered was sitting in a brooding silence near Mr Lambert, ostensibly helping to keep watch. Now I was in a horizontal position, on my side, with my head resting on someone's folded coat.

'Gobble, gobble!'

I turned my head. A large light brown and perfectly round eye stared at me, and I cowered back in alarm.

Hoots of laughter drowned out the gobbles emitting from the long throat of the emu, for such was the owner of that inquisitive eye, the tall flightless bird led so often to its doom by its curiosity. Jem had told me that these creatures were killed and captured quite easily by aboriginals playing upon this peculiar weakness.

'Go away!' I cried, scrambling to my feet and flinging away my blanket. The emu, standing seventy inches from large feet to tiny head, after one more twist of its neck to see me the better, decided to retreat.

'Shoo!' I added, waving my arms, and it broke into an awkward trot, soon vanishing amidst the trees behind us.

The men had had their joke at my expense, and I hastily combed my ugly short hair and, womanlike, tried to make myself a little more presentable, although I had scant desire to impress any one of this disreputable trio.

'Mick has caught some fish,' announced Mr Lambert, indicating a small but sufficient number of fish which lay on a heap of clean leaves, awaiting the pan.

It was a welcome change from the quite unpalatable food which had been our fare at the hands of Isaac Purtle, who fancied himself, without cause, as a capable camp cook. Even the strong, black tea, stewed up in a quart pot on an open fire, and always tasting more of smoke than of leaves, was acceptable after such a good breakfast. I felt that the day had started brightly and, observing that he was in a good humour, I asked Mr Lambert why he had not awakened me to finish sharing our watch.

'I wanted some peace,' he replied. He did not mention what he had discussed with me under the stars only a few hours before. If he had made a decision regarding his search for the lost white woman, he kept it to himself, and by half past eight, we had mounted up and were on our way. Once again the vegetation changed, to fields of sedge and reeds and patches of salt marsh, where the succulents spread carpet-like over the soggy earth, opening up their small purple flowers amidst the varying tones of their squashy leaves. Birds flew away at our approach, the birds of the water, small white and grey birds resembling our European swifts, plovers, stilts, white ibises, curlews, terns, gulls, sandpipers, ducks arising startled in a great flock, and past the reeds, etched on the open waters of the deeper parts of this lagoon, a great number of black swans.

Mr Lambert looked back over his shoulder, to the westwards, anxiously.

'Let's get across,' he announced. 'I don't think the weather's going to hold.'

The sun shone brilliantly, but there were dark streaks across the lower skies, and there was a sort of shimmer in the light. We all lost our happy mood, and settled down to the task of finding our way across

175

the lagoon. This part of the shallow lake constituted a sort of border region between the waters emptied into it from small rivers at its western end, and the overflow from the main lakes of the system. There were slimy sand islets dotted across, and as the water was no more than inches deep, we were soon across without mishap. Now we were a mere few hundred yards from the high tree-covered dunes which separated us from the beach.

'Are you sure this is the place?' Mr Lambert asked Mick in a nervous, excited voice, and now the Maori's place in this bizarre expedition became apparent. In some way, he had knowledge of the spot where Mrs Lambert had last been seen.

'Won't know until we're across the hills,' said Mick, dragging the unwilling pack horse from tussock to tussock across a bog from which mosquitoes swarmed in millions. Several wallabies bounded away from the noise we made, and the blue and red parrots screeched warnings to the whole bush as they fled from one tree top to another.

Isaac Purtle rode alongside myself, leaning over to guide my horse when it baulked at yet another swampy patch.

'How does the Maori know where to go?' I asked.

' 'E was on the ship. The one Mrs Lambert was on.' Isaac kept leaning towards me after the need had passed. 'Don't understand much what it's all about meself. Never seen Mr Lambert so set on anythin', and 'e's a man what when 'e makes up 'is mind, 'e goes through with it. 'E worshipped the ground under 'er feet, and 'e won't give up 'opin' she's still alive.'

'And what do you think?' I had a feeling of elation inside of me. Isaac Purtle was a basically honest man, and my instinct that he liked me had been correct. Now I had to make sure that he was my ally, when and if the need arose.

'I think she's dead, miss. Mick is sure she is. But Mr Lambert now — and 'im what's always bin so 'ardheaded — 'e's got some bee in his bonnet. All I 'ope is . . . ' He broke off, as if he had said too much.

'What do you hope, Mr Purtle?' I asked, silkily, and I think that it was the 'Mr Purtle,' a piece of politeness he seldom heard, which softened him.

'We don't all end up in Van Diemen's Land. I don't fancy becomin' a canary[1] at my age, miss. Like I told you, I was a

---

[1] That is a convict, because of yellow clothing.

soldier, until the drink ruined me. It was Mr Lambert what gave me a chance agin. 'E's a real gentleman, miss, an' never you doubt it.'

I thought of that 'real gentleman' striking me across the face, and then, as if to counterbalance this, I unwillingly remembered awakening that morning to find my head comfortably pillowed on a rolled up coat. Sorting out Mr Lambert became more difficult as each day passed.

'How odd,' I said, eager to keep Isaac talking. 'I mean, you've been a free man all your life, and yet you work for one who was a prisoner.'

'Well, 'e don't like to be reminded of it, miss. 'E's got a conditional pardon, and there's the rub. 'E'd like to retire to England. 'E's rich enough, but 'e goes out o' New South Wales, and 'e loses 'is pardon. Mr Eldridge — Mrs Lambert's father — had friends in 'igh places, and he arranged to get Mr Lambert let off the rest of 'is sentence. Mr Lambert was transported for fourteen years, but 'e served no more 'n four years all told. Old Mr Eldridge reckoned it was wrong, and got up petitions and wrote to England, but a conditional pardon was the best they could do. Pity of it is, since then those coves sent out from Dorset, the

Tolpuddle Martyrs, they called 'em in the broadsheets, all got free pardons and their slates wiped clean.'

Mr Lambert and Maori Mick had pulled up on higher ground, and were waiting for us with an air of great impatience. But I had to ask another question. Once again, my picture was becoming badly distorted, with the perspective quite out of focus. Mr Lambert and Mr Eldridge had once, obviously, been friends. What had been the cause of the falling out which had prompted Mrs Lambert's father to make such a will as to ensure that Quentin Lambert could not inherit, even indirectly?

'Why was Mr Lambert transported?' I asked. When I had first arrived in Australia, the subject of the Tolpuddle Martyrs had still been much discussed, for, after long legal battles, their sentences had been rescinded and they had been given free passage back to Britain. Their crime had been in forming a society to seek, collectively, better wages for farm labourers. I had always assumed that Mr Lambert had been convicted for embezzlement, or a similar offence, and this talk of the Dorset men confused me.

' 'E was one of them crazy rick-burners,' said Isaac Purtle, leaving me to follow as he urged his mount forward.

14

It was hard to fit Mr Lambert, so cool and calculating, into the mould of a rick-burner. He was cynical and ruthless, and it was hard, nay impossible, to think of him, even in the silliest days of his youth, doing anything as futile and liable to punishment as rick-burning. Rick-burners were dangerous and hot-headed men, rather like my own father had been, before dissipation had sapped his idealism.

I had, of course, been a child in a foreign country during this ugly part of our history, when starving farmhands, trying to bring their plight before those who ruled the land, had embarked on a course of arson and destruction, often being hanged or transported for their pains. They were the extremists, the mad ones who saw wanton havoc as the path to reform, and their activities had sent a shudder of fear through a country still recovering from the long wars which had followed the French Revolution.

Still, there was no time to muse over Isaac Purtle's amazing revelation, for we could hear the surf pounding thunderously against the beach, which was no more than a few hundred feet distant, yet separated from us by a natural barrier of thick scrub.

'There must be a place where the blacks walk through,' said Mr Lambert, after we had ridden about a mile along the inland base of the dunes, vainly searching for an easy way.

'The tea tree is a bit thinner over that way,' announced Isaac Purtle. 'There's bin a fire through by the looks of it.'

So, once again, the poor horses were forced on, stumbling and slipping in the loose sand which slid away from beneath their hooves, so that we had to dismount and tug them up to the crest. Now the waves crashing against the beach were almost deafening as we emerged from the charred tea tree and stared down through a gap in the last hummocks. I was not prepared for the beauty of this desolate place as our faces were met by the rush of cold air from the ocean.

The sand on the wide beach — it was low tide — was the colour of gold, and stretched as far as the eye could reach in either direction, until it disappeared in a haze of spray from the surf. Near the shore, the water was a deep green, and further out, an intense blue, topped by the white foam of breakers. This was the coast where the waters of Bass Strait met the Pacific Ocean, and it was as if both were at constant war, meeting, surging, and merciless. The last high tide had left a miniature cliff in the sand, about a yard high, and we lined up along this, gripping the horses' bridles, and awaiting our leader's next move.

Mr Lambert took out his map, and dropped to his knees, holding the paper firmly against the breeze. Behind the dunes, it had been mild and warm, but now I shivered, and wished for the pea jacket wrapped up in my blanket.

'We should be about two miles west of the place,' he said, waving a hand vaguely in the other direction. 'I think we'd best stick to the beach. It would be easier.'

'I don't like the looks o' the weather,' grumbled Isaac Purtle, and I agreed with him. A solid line of black was moving up steadily behind the few clouds I had noticed earlier.

'Whatever we do won't change it,' snapped Mr Lambert. 'I want to see the spot.'

So we mounted again, and cantered along the firm sand, while the clouds rose behind us and the sun still warmed us a little against the cold salt-spray. We passed a place where the first line of dunes had been almost flattened, and beyond that I could see a great stretch of bleached shells, like those of cockles.

'That's where the blacks 've been 'avin' their feasts,' Isaac told me. More than ever, he seemed to have taken me under his wing. 'Them's what they call pipis. At the right time, you can stand on the edge of the surf and see 'em 'oppin' up with the waves. Next wave, they'll burrow back into the sand, quick as a wink. The blacks 'old bags in their teeth, and what with grabbin' some and diggin' for some, they soon 'as enough for a feed.'

Maori Mick, who was ahead, drew rein, and pointed up to a particularly high dune, well covered by scrubby vegetation, where three spars had been pushed hard into the sand and then lashed together at the top to form a triangular marker. Mr Lambert pulled up his own horse short, and stared up at the spars, the part of his face visible between his growing beard and the brim of his hat deathly white. Isaac jumped down from his own horse, his ugly face frowning and anxious.

Mick turned back in his saddle, and pointed to the edge of the surf with a fat brown finger.

'There, Mr Lambert.'

One could see, just exposed by the tide,

a piece of mahogany-coloured timber, briefly revealed as the waves flowed and ebbed. That was all, one heavy piece of wood from the ill-fated ship, and those three spars high on the dunes. This, then, was what we had come all this way to see. Nothing worth the journey.

The sun was blotted out, suddenly, and the first drops of rain began to fall. We all hurried back to the dunes, seeking shelter from the fierce squall which swirled sand along the beach and whipped up the breakers into a crashing anger. My horse decided to go in another direction, and by the time I had caught up with the others, who were huddled beneath some trees, I was drenched. Mr Lambert sent me a disgusted look, intimating that such stupidity was all that could be expected of me.

Eventually, the squall passed, and a little watery sunshine emerged, although the summery warmth of the early morning had quite passed away. I was shivering in my damp clothes as we returned to the beach, and Mr Lambert must have pitied me. He decided that whilst Maori Mick explained to him exactly what had happened when the survivors had struggled ashore through the powerful undertow, lucky to escape the sharks which infested these waters, I should stay on the sheltered side of the dune which formed a bulwark against the beach.

The horses were tethered to some stunted trees which had managed to grow in the loose sand of the dunes, and I crouched down nearby in a sort of alcove, wishing that I could change my clothes. I longed for a hot tub with a good supply of warmed, freshly laundered towels. I remembered all the clucking and fussing which went on when I was a child and was accidentally caught in a rainstorm. Alida or Elinora or Sophia, or whoever happened to be our housekeeper at the time, would immediately fill a great wooden tub, and I would be divested of my clothing and popped therein, to be warmed — nearly boiled sometimes — and then rubbed down briskly. In those days, I was precious and wanted and loved, not a pawn in some sinister, inexplicable game, shivering to my grave behind a heap of sand in God-forsaken Gipps Land.

Mr Lambert and Maori Mick raised their voices, and I peered over the rim of the dune. The wind was still blowing strongly, and the three men huddled against its force, while the waves, the tide having turned, were lashing up the beach towards the bank which marked the last high tide.

'Where did you see her last? Show me

the place!' This was Mr Lambert, clutching at his hat, his coat flapping about his wiry body, demanding to the point of fury.

Maori Mick, with his large, solid form turned against the wind, seemed to have lost his usual good humour.

'Mrs Lambert was sick. We made her sit there against the sandhill — ' he pointed to the low mound behind which I was crouched — 'and we went up there to see what we could.' And he indicated the high dune with the spars.

'You shouldn't have left her alone,' cried Mr Lambert, above the sound of the waves.

'We needed our bearings. We wasn't gone long.'

How many souls had been snatched from their bodies when the ship had crashed into a reef, unseen, somewhere out there where the blue had changed to green? Four poor wretches had been cast ashore in this wild place, one of them a frail woman. Four out of how many? No wonder mariners feared this southern coast of New South Wales, where the wild storms could sweep a stout vessel off course, to crash it against the rocky islands of the Straits, or throw it against the sands of the Ninety Mile Beach.

'And when we come back, Mrs Lambert was gone.'

'Gone? Why should she go?'

Mr Lambert's utterance was not so much a question as a cry of anguish. His wife had been here, alive and breathing, and in a few short moments she had disappeared. I know where she went, I thought, cold again as the sun vanished behind another heavy cloud. She climbed up over to this side to find some relief from the wind.

'We looked, Mr Lambert. As I believe in Jesus Christ, Our Lord, we looked!' The tattooed New Zealander was imploring the other, so obsessed by his quest, not to be angry, while Isaac Purtle, suddenly making up his mind, trudged up towards the spars high on the big dune, which was some distance to my right as I sat there with my back to the beach.

Now, what faced me was a relatively flat and open space, narrowing to my left to skirt an eroded dune and then widening out again into that great expanse of bleached pipi shells which I had seen earlier. The coastal range had been worn away at this point by the sheer pressure of many black feet over countless centuries, and by the action of the wind on dunes from which growth had been torn to provide fuel for fires. About fifty yards directly in front of me was a line of demarcation, where the sand blowing in from this bare open patch was engaged in battle with trees and undergrowth trying to fight their way back from the inland side.

Perhaps, I thought, she was thirsty and wandered off, looking for water. She must have walked across to the trees, and her footprints would have been obliterated almost immediately if the wind was at all stronger than it is today.

Then, startled, I stared at the unbelievably ugly old black crone who had emerged from the trees, carrying a woven basket and wearing nothing but a tattered old fur rug about her wrinkled person. Amidst the native people of New South Wales, the women are always smaller than the men, not as amongst our own race, who vary so much in size, regardless of sex. Maybe because they have to make do with the food left after their masters have eaten, they inevitably age faster than the male blacks, who often retain a good physique far longer than white men of comparative age. Those poor native women seem to be little more than beasts of burden, and when they shift camp, as they frequently must in their wild condition, the man strides ahead unencumbered except for his weapons, whilst his small harem struggle after, literally bent over under their loads of rugs, spare weapons, dishes, baskets, fishing nets, perhaps a baby, and in addition grasping digging sticks in case they see something which can be garnered for food. One of the women is entrusted with the fire stick, a piece of wood smouldering at one end, so that there will be no necessity to enact the wearisome business of making a fresh flame by friction, and woe betide any lubra who lets that precious glow die. She is beaten with a severity which could kill a British woman.

As well as her finely woven basket, this old woman had in her grasp the usual digging stick, so that yams and other vegetable oddments could be prised from the soil. It could also be used to dig out small animals and reptiles to add to the day's menu.

There was no thought of food gathering now in the lubra's tousled grey head. She was paralysed by fear, her big eyes wide and her lips trembling. Then, she let out a shrill squawk, and fled back into the shelter of the scrub, dropping her stick and her basket in her flight. As much as anything, I was astonished, for one small and effeminate youth could not have been expected to cause such fear.

'What's wrong? Did you call out?'

It was Mr Lambert, leaping energetically

over the sand to my side, and quickly I explained.

'Oh, was that all?' he said, but then Isaac Purtle joined us.

'The old woman was scared out of her wits by miss here,' he said. 'I seen it all from up there.' He nodded back towards the high sandhill with the spars. 'There's a camp o' theirs back o' the hills 'ere. She's most likely bringin' 'er friends to 'ave a look at us.'

'Perhaps she thought that we're hunting for the blacks who killed the shepherd,' I interrupted.

'Don't think so, miss. Could be, but . . .' He hesitated, and looked at Mr Lambert queryingly.

'Well, out with it!' ordered our leader, impatiently, at the same time looking towards the scrub none too easily.

'I reckon the lubra thought miss 'ere was a ghost. You know as well as meself that miss looks like Mrs Lambert 'cept for 'er 'air. The blacks, miss, believe in ghosts. There was a man, William Buckley was 'is name, now 'e lived with the blacks over Melbourne way nigh on thirty years. He got stranded, and they'd 'ave killed 'im, only they thought 'e was the spirit of one of themselves that'd just died, 'cos, 'e looked like their friend.'

It had started to rain again, lightly, and I sneezed. Mr Lambert seemed not to notice. He was thinking very hard.

'All right,' he said then, 'bring the horses down on to the beach. We'll wait there. If they start throwing their spears at us, we'll be off for our lives. But you're right, Isaac. There's a chance they'll come to look at Miss Smith.'

So we waited, in the cold wind and intermittent rain, while the poor horses bent their heads and whinnied complainingly from time to time. We had to move once as the sea slithered up the beach about our horses' legs, but then, after nearly an hour, we were rewarded. A very big aboriginal man, taller than most of his fellows, appeared on the dunes above us.

'They've been watching us,' muttered Isaac. 'Makin' up their minds if we're goin' to shoot them.'

'See if you can talk to him,' said Mr Lambert, imperturbably.

Isaac slid his gun, which he had been holding low, behind his horse, across to Maori Mick, and walked out boldly towards the black man, who was the first wild black I had ever seen at close quarters. The ones back at the Reeds' had been well tamed and trained into wearing clothes, but this one had

191

nought but his cloak, made, I think, from wallaby skins with the fur on the outside, and with a little of an incised pattern on the inside showing. His long hair was caught up in a kind of a bun on the top of his head, and kept from falling by a finely woven band about his forehead. His colouring was not black, but nearer grey, this being caused by the smearing of his body with a mixture of fat and ashes, by which means these people protected themselves from the cold and insect bites. He carried two spears, made from fine, heat-straightened saplings, and a heavy club or waddy, these being his usual hunting implements.

Isaac Purtle made a gesture and then, producing the inevitable plug of tobacco, held it out towards the savage. The man still looked both surly and suspicious. These Gipps Land blacks may have been in an isolated part of New South Wales, but they had had considerable experience of white men. Sealers had been landing along their shores for half a century, taking women as they pleased, and as sealers were usually the dregs of the white race, there was little liking for Europeans in the hearts of the aboriginals.

The black man spoke, and pointed towards me. Isaac made it plain that he did not understand, and after a few moments, the savage left his perch up by the spars, and disappeared back into the sandhills.

'We'll go,' said Mr Lambert, glancing towards me. 'I don't like this.'

''Ang on, guv'nor,' said Isaac Purtle, 'I reckons I was right. It was miss he was interested in.'

This time, we did not have to wait very long. The big aboriginal reappeared, with a youngish lubra, who, for her race, was quite attractive, especially when she smiled. She spoke some broken English.

Although she glanced coquettishly towards us, being fully aware of her charms, the man was very much in command. He held out his hand for his tobacco, which Isaac gave to him, and things having been established on a business footing, the questions could now be asked. The lubra, it transpired, had not been born a member of the local tribe, having come from near Melbourne after being snatched during a raid. Isaac asked her why her people were so frightened of us and why they hid themselves. She replied that white men were crazy. When a black man wished to avenge himself for one death, he killed one man. The whites killed everyone they saw.

This conversation between her and Isaac

was not carried on in speech only, but with the aid of signs and drawings in the sand. Isaac did not press things too hard. He told her that we had no ill intentions towards her people, and were not interested in who had murdered the shepherd near the Bruthen Creek.

That was nothing to do with her people, she declared. The bad blacks from the mountains had killed the shepherd, who anyway was a cruel man and deserved it. She did not explain the extraordinary fact that it had taken us over two days hard riding on horseback to reach this place, but the news of the shepherd's death had gone before us. This all being settled, Isaac now asked whether she knew anything of a white woman said to be living amongst the blacks.

There was a rapid interchange of talk between her and the man. Mention of the white woman had upset them both, we could see, but after some debate, she turned back to us. Her husband, she said, was Bungelene, who was a very powerful man amongst the Kurnai people. He liked tobacco very much.

Mr Lambert sighed, and found some more tobacco.

Isaac now asked the leading question. Why

had the old woman been so frightened when she had seen the boy? He pointed towards me, and the lubra spoke to Bungelene in their own language, while the big aboriginal's face settled into sullen and anxious lines.

'Tell him,' said Mr Lambert urgently, 'that we're looking for a white woman whose face was like that of the boy. She came ashore here from the sea.'

Isaac explained this in his mixture of words and signs, and now the lubra appeared distressed as she talked rapidly to her master. I felt a quickening of excitement. They knew about Mrs Lambert! I was positive, and so was Mr Lambert.

'Tell him,' said Isaac, pointing to the surly Bungelene, who was more than ready to break off the discussion and retreat back into the bush, 'that we don't want to hurt any of you. We're not police.'

'The woman was my woman,' interrupted Mr Lambert, 'I must know where she is.'

The lubra stared straight at me.

'That's your woman,' she said distinctly, and her big white teeth flashed provocatively in her black face.

Mr Lambert did not miss a beat, although I felt absolutely mortified that this primitive creature could have seen through a disguise which had deceived Mr Nesbitt.

'She isn't my woman. My woman looks like her. Have you seen my woman?'

Now, there was a hasty palaver between the two blacks, and Bungelene stepped forward and gripped my arm, and touched my face, and tugged my hair.

'She ain't a ghost,' growled Isaac. 'Now, where's the dead woman?'

Bungelene may not have been able to understand the words, but he heard the threat in Isaac's voice, and with a growling mutter, he stepped back and brandished his club. The woman caught at his arm, while Mr Lambert reached for his pistols.

'Not hurt woman,' cried the lubra, despairingly. 'She sick. She die.'

Fear came from the pair of them like a scent. Poor creatures, they were harried in a land which had been theirs for thousands of years.

'I know she was sick.' Mr Lambert spoke placatingly. 'Where did she die? I must see the place.'

There was a hurried translation, and Bungelene considered for a few moments. He would show us the body, he announced, through the woman, but he would have to be paid. Mr Lambert agreed. He would give them a blanket. The lubra then acted out Mrs Lambert's last minutes on earth.

Now, our meeting with these particular people was not such a coincidence as it may seem. The clans of the Kurnai, although nomadic like all the aboriginals, had no need to wander as far in search of food as other less fortunate tribes. The waters of the lakes teemed with fish, and the reedy shores were the nesting places of huge flocks of wild duck. Game abounded all about, as did the items which made up the vegetable part of an aboriginal's diet. They had been in the locality when we had made camp the previous night, and had followed us out of curiosity.

On the day of Mrs Lambert's death, Bungelene's two wives, our informant and the old woman who had been so frightened, and some other women of the tribe, had been searching for mushrooms. One of the children had scampered away towards the beach, and had come back with the story that there was a white woman sitting in the dunes. They had gone to investigate, and when the woman had seen them, she had risen to her feet, and staggered towards them, obviously in great distress.

Like all her race, our young lubra was a clever mimic, and as she acted this out, helped along by her few words of English, I saw that Mr Lambert's face was so still, and so wooden that I knew he was fighting to keep control of himself. We formed a sort of triangle as we followed the lubra, with Mr Lambert at the front, and the three others keeping a few cautious paces to the rear, for none of us really trusted Bungelene, and Isaac muttered to us that he was sure there were other black men amidst the trees nearby.

Mrs Lambert had reached the trees beyond the open expanse of sand when her ebbing life had left her, to collapse and die at the feet of the bewildered black women and their children. They heard the voices of the white men calling from the high dune, and having already had experience of the justice meted out when white lives or property were injured, they had acted quickly to protect themselves. Our lubra informant, clever and fast-thinking, had told the others to hide the body in the sand, and she herself had, while the white men were scrambling clumsily from the top of the high dune (she had not seen them closely enough to know that one was a Maori), run forth and back with a branch to obliterate those footprints which had not already been buried by the wind.

Thus had Mrs Lambert disappeared, and now she was to be uncovered. Mr Lambert knelt down and began to dig in the soft sand beneath the grey branches of dead tea tree which had been dragged over the spot.

'Turn yer back, miss,' said Isaac in my ear, and then Mr Lambert arose and staggered away, too overcome to continue in his gruesome, self-appointed task. Maori Mick eventually uncovered Mrs Lambert's remains, and later, about two hours before sunset, she was more decently interred in firm ground well behind the sandhills.

The blacks watched from a distance, and Isaac had been right in his surmise that there had been others than Bungelene and his two women nearby. This time it was Maori Mick who recited a service of sorts, made up of the Lord's Prayer and a part of the Twenty-third Psalm. I gathered some wild flowers and placed them upon the grave, while Mr Lambert, tears rolling down his cheeks, watched me.

I felt a surge of pity, and a desire to do something to help him in this moment of sorrow, and quite forgetting all our past frictions and my usual opinion of him, I asked whether he would lend me his notebook and pencil. He was surprised, but too shocked, I think, to argue.

I sat on a fallen tree trunk, and sketched the glade in which Mrs Lambert had been laid to her final rest. When I handed him the result, he stared down at my little drawing, and then at me, his tawny brows drawing together.

'Why, you're an excellent artist!' he exclaimed. 'Thank you, Miss Smith. I'll treasure this. Now we must be on our way while there's still daylight. I don't trust our black friends.'

So, the day which had begun with merriment as I was awakened by the emu, ended sadly, with the four of us riding along the beach towards Port Albert, fifty miles away. The first part of Mr Lambert's enterprise was concluded.

15

For Mr Lambert, speed had now become all important. He had to carry through his deception quickly, before any other searchers produced a captive white woman. My feeling of sympathy for him soon evaporated as he forced us back towards Port Albert, this time carefully avoiding any chance of encountering white settlers by keeping close to the beach, riding over sandhills which exhausted us almost as much as the horses. This course exposed us to all the sudden changes in weather which were typical of this part of New South Wales, and to add to our miseries, our food ran very short. Maori Mick shot two wild ducks which no one quite knew how to cook, and they were so tough that the effort of eating them was hardly worth the while. Chewing at a stringy leg, I decided that here, surely was the reason why the Australian aboriginal people have such large strong teeth.

When, at last, the smoke from Port Albert's few chimneys could be seen wavering above the scrub, Mr Lambert called a halt. The first thing he did was to send Maori Mick ahead to buy provisions, and Isaac Purtle instantly grumbled about this, declaring that he had more idea of striking a bargain than that Bible-thumping heathen.

'I can trust Mick to walk past a public house,' said Mr Lambert, laconically, as he busied himself with our poor, tired pack horse.

I wondered why we could not all proceed into Port Albert, which, to me, now represented comfort and civilisation. For the past twenty-four hours I had not been feeling well. The rough conditions tried me severely, and I had caught a chill upon that day when we had found Elizabeth Lambert's body. My feeling of malaise had been considerably heightened by a resurgence of my morbid fancies. It had become my conviction that death was my constant attendant, and that if I had not been with them, Mr Lambert and his companions may have found his wife alive. As I sat wearily with my back against a tree awaiting Mick's return, I did not yet realise that the strains upon my senses, which had commenced with that ill-fated visit to the Neapolitan witch, had mounted until I was almost at breaking point.

Mr Lambert approached me, holding a small bottle in one hand.

'Miss Smith,' he said, 'the time has come

for you to earn your hundred pounds. We're going to dye your hair.'

Staring back at him with all the defiance I could muster, I knew that it was little use arguing, for I was caught up so thoroughly in his machinations that submission was the only course. So, my poor hair, which had grown a little but was far from the glory it had been, was submitted to the further indignity of being doused with dark brown dye. Then, from the pack Mr Lambert produced a skirt. It was a horrid skirt, a drab brown colour (to match my hair?), and far from new and certainly not clean.

'No,' I said. I had grown to like my boyish garb, which was comfortable, and which, I flattered myself, rather suited me. A crisp and dainty dress would have lured me out of my breeches, but this tattered garment made me wrinkle up my nose in disgust. For the first time in several days, Mr Lambert laughed.

'Come on, now,' he coaxed, 'don't spoil your looks by pulling faces. I'll admit that you look rather charming dressed as a boy, but we've work afoot.'

'You have. I want no part of it.' For the first time, it had occurred to me that Mr Lambert *needed* me. He would not hurt me. Not now.

'All right,' he said mildly. 'In the morning then, before we go into Port Albert.'

'But I thought we were moving on into Port Albert this afternoon,' I cried. Words cannot describe how I longed for that miserable little settlement, with its few huts and shacks, and its promise of something resembling a real bed. I had a headache and a sore throat, and all manner of aches and pains.

'We were, but I'm going to give you a few extra hours to recover from your sulks.'

I grabbed the skirt and retired behind some trees to change, and when I emerged, it was to find Mr Lambert deep in conversation with Isaac Purtle and Mick, who had returned from his errand. They all turned as I approached, and Isaac Purtle stepped forward, holding out his hand to me.

'Well, miss,' he said, 'it's goodbye for the time bein'. Must say that when the Guv'nor said you was comin' with us on this lark, I 'ad me doubts. But you're a real little lady.'

I allowed him to shake my hand, heartily, although I could feel only trepidation. Somehow, I had depended upon Isaac staying with us, but now I was to learn that he and Mick were leaving us to return to Sydney, overland. Mr Lambert's planning had been careful down to the last detail. To return to Port Albert with the same party and a female instead of his 'nephew' would have aroused comment and outright suspicion. The 'nephew' would be said to have gone off with the others, and only myself and Mr Lambert would come in from the wilds.

'An' mind you looks after 'er, Mr Lambert,' added Isaac to his employer.

'I think Miss Smith can look after herself,' was the chilling answer.

In saying good-bye Maori Mick told me that he would pray for the success of our plans, which gave me no great faith in the extent of his conversion. Within a few minutes, they were both mounted up and, leading the pack horse and the mare which had been my own steed, were soon off towards McMillan's track, which would lead them to Flooding Creek on the first leg of their long journey.

'I'm afraid you'll have to enter Port Albert up behind me,' murmured Mr Lambert, removing the silk scarf he wore knotted about his neck. 'Still, if my nephew had to return to Sydney overland, he needed his horse. Here, cover your hair with this.' And he tossed me the scarf.

'Why?' I asked. 'I thought you wanted people to think that I was Mrs Lambert.'

'Ha,' he said, with that crafty light very

apparent in his glowing brown eyes. 'Ha. When one sets out to deceive, Miss Smith, one must not be obvious. Whatever you are asked, you must say that I'm escorting you to Melbourne. You're a servant girl who's found life in Gipps Land too rough, and you're being sent back to town.'

I took the scarf and fastened it over my head in the manner of the peasant women I remembered from my childhood, while he watched me, head cocked slightly to one side.

'You're very flushed,' he observed. 'Are you feeling quite well?'

'I'm perfectly well,' I lied, determined not to show the smallest sign of weakness.

Ten minutes later, sitting behind Mr Lambert on his horse and clutching him about the waist, I had to resist the urge to lay my hot cheek against his back, for by now my head was aching almost intolerably.

Our arrival at Port Albert caused a noticeable stirring of interest. The harbour master who doubled up as undertaker and almost everything else, the publican and his wife and three barefoot children, a couple of men who lived in a humpy on the beach, the storekeeper, and a cattleman who happened to be 'in town' from his nearby run, all stared at us, full of conjecture, but too polite to ask.

They remembered Mr Lambert sufficiently to address him by name, and undoubtedly they knew that he had set forth from Port Albert, within the past fortnight, to search for that elusive white woman.

At the public house, he asked civily for some overnight accommodation for the young lady. That ship out in the harbour, now, was it bound for Melbourne?

No, it was off across the Bass Straits to Launceston in Van Diemen's Land, and due to up anchor as soon as the cattle were aboard. The steamer from Melbourne was due any day now, and high time, too, with provisions running low again.

I was shown to a miserable little cell, hardly large enough to hold a sagging bedstead, and the publican's wife loitered, bursting with curiosity. Well schooled on the way from our last camp, I said that I had come from past Flooding Creek and was returning to Melbourne for the sake of my health.

'H'm,' she said, plainly forming her own opinion. 'Women's so scarce in these parts it's a marvel you weren't married off soon as you got to Flooding Creek.'

'I've a fiancé in Melbourne,' I answered, and could see that this puzzled her. Too late, I gathered that I did not sound like a semi-literate servant girl. I had also erred in using the word, 'fiancé.' It was far too grand for the person I was supposed to be, and yet, by this mistake, I actually helped Mr Lambert by arousing more conjecture about my identity.

When I was alone, I lay down on the lumpy bed, and stared up at the ceiling, which was made of hessian stretched under the beams. Here and there, stains showed where water had dripped through the shingles, and this increased my wretchedness. Nothing in my life was right, and I knew, in one of those moments of clarity and self-revelation which come when a human being has reached the nadir, that nothing was going to be right. Even supposing that I came through this adventure without being convicted, there was still that warrant for my arrest. When I had extricated myself from Mr Lambert's plot and finally found my way to Jem, what would be his reaction? Most likely, he would have already had a letter from the Reeds about me, and if he had not, how could I explain my sudden arrival with cropped, dyed hair and one hundred pounds? Would Jem be willing to throw away his promising start in New South Wales for my sake? Could I expect it of him?

Running away had always added to my troubles, and repeating the process could only cause more problems. When my father's wife had made her terrible accusations, I should have fought back, but I had been too young, too frightened, and . . . too guilty.

I sat up and swung my legs to the floor, strangely encumbered by my skirts after the freedom of trousers. My illness was fast overcoming me, but, dizzy as I was, my resolution was unimpaired. Impulsive and foolish I had been, but I was no criminal, and I had had sufficient of helping that wily ex-rick-burner defraud his father-in-law's legal heirs. And if it all ended with my arrest and deportation back to England — that was my destiny. Abruptly, I thought of Mr Ellett, the young man who had been in charge of my half-brothers. He had made it very clear at the time that he was my friend. I felt sure, now, looking back, that he would have supported me. It was my memory now of that handsome and good man which gave me the impetus I needed to take me out of the public house and search for the harbour master, who was the only person of official standing in Port Albert at that time.

There was no sign of Mr Lambert in the main street, if that cleared strip with a few tree stumps still protruding here and there could be graced by such a title, and I ventured towards the beach. A man who was tending the cattle in the crudely fenced yards turned and called out to me.

'Hullo, lubra!' he jeered. 'What about a kiss for a white man for a change?'

Before I could hurry away, this person had jumped the fence and was at my side, smirking down at me.

'Go away,' I said. He was dirty, the dirtiness of a very long abstinence from washing, and smelled strongly of spirits.

'Hoity toity, ain't we? Turnin' up yer nose at a white man, eh? We'll soon put that to rights.'

He grabbed me, and began kissing me roughly, and as I struggled, I heard what sounded like a great explosion. I was released as suddenly as I had been seized, and saw Mr Lambert standing a few feet away, holding in one hand the still smoking pistol he had fired into the air. I remember thinking how strange it was that, during our quest for Elizabeth Lambert, he had not fired one shot in anger, but here, not two hours after reaching civilisation, he had been forced to do so.

'The next time,' he said, quietly, shifting that pistol to his left hand and opening his coat to show its partner still in his belt, 'I won't fire into the air. Come on, Miss Smith.'

People had come running, and he told

them, curtly, that he had fired at a wild dog. Crestfallen, I followed him as he stalked back towards the public house, and after several yards, he stopped, and took my arm.

'You fool,' he said. 'Why didn't you have the sense to stay inside?'

'I'm going to the harbour master,' I said, my head whirling with fever and distaste at my recent experience. 'I'm going to tell him the whole story. I *won't* have men thinking I've been living like a savage. You can do what you like, but I'm not going to help you.'

'You've left this awakening of conscience rather late, haven't you?' Mr Lambert, plainly afraid that I was going to make a scene in the middle of the street, tried to hurry me on, but I stood still, determined to make my feelings clear.

'I'm no criminal,' I stated. 'I'm not going to risk a term in Van Diemen's Land for you.'

He swatted at a mosquito, and appeared to think over what I had said.

'And neither am I a criminal,' he announced. 'If I thought I could trust you, my mysterious little Miss Smith, I'd tell you the truth.'

Trust me? The truth? What did he mean? As I tried to think of an answer, a shadow fell on the ground between us, and then

I saw the flash of the sinking sun on a knife blade as my would-be ravisher jumped between us, his weapon raised to strike Mr Lambert, who, with reflexes as swift as those of the animal which had given him a nickname, swerved to one side. The big stockman moved about swiftly, trying to thrust the knife into Mr Lambert, and, hardly hearing the yells of those running to this unexpected entertainment, I picked up a large piece of wood which lay on the ground. It was meant for a fence, I think, being quite heavy, and grasping it with both hands, I made a tremendous effort and hit fiercely in the direction of the man with the knife. At that instant, he had ducked to dodge Mr Lambert's fists, and at the same time he thrust upwards with his knife, to be felled as my club hit him on the back of the head, just above his collar.

The whole population of Port Albert had now arrived, and someone knelt down by the inert body, and I felt myself sinking into a horror of blackness. The old Italian's prophecy had been fulfilled. Now I was truly lost. I had killed another human being.

'Catch hold of her. She's fainting.'

The warning came to me from an immense distance, someone put their arms about me, and I knew no more.

16

It was a real bed, with clean linen sheets and plumped up pillows, in a small but spotless room, and I was lying in it. I did not know where the room might be, but I could see, as I looked out of the window, that it was upstairs in a house built on a slight eminence, because I could see a river with ships at anchor, and rising land beyond, with white dots, which I guessed were recently shorn sheep, scattered upon the green sward.

How long had I been here? The hand which lay limply upon the turned back portion of the sheet was thin and white almost to transparency, and I was still regarding it, trying to recall the events which had brought me here, when the door opened and a pleasant-looking woman of about thirty-five came into the bedroom. When she saw me, her face lit up with delight.

'You're awake! And feeling better? Oh, I'm so glad. Quentin is away today, but what a relief it'll be to him to find you a little recovered!'

'How long have I been here? Where am I?'

By Quentin, this stranger meant Mr Lambert, who had dragged me off to the wilds of Gipps Land, where — my poor mind, still struggling to adjust itself — refused to go any further. Something terrible had happened. What?

'You've been here for two weeks, and desperately ill for three. Quentin brought you by ship from Port Albert. You're in Melbourne now, and I'm Quentin's cousin, Grace Hanley.'

I saw that she wore a wedding ring, which made her Mrs Hanley. This little effort had quite exhausted me, and now I sank back on to my pillows and drifted once more into sleep. When I again awoke, it was dark, and Mrs Hanley came into the room carrying a lighted lamp, which she placed upon the tiny table at my bedside.

'Now,' she said, in that idiotically cheerful voice which so many people use when addressing invalids, 'you'll no doubt feel like eating a little supper.'

As she spoke, there came back into my mind the vision of that last moment before I had slipped into the dark mists amidst which I had dwelt for the past three weeks. I had killed a man. I was a murderess. Why I should be here in this clean and comfortable bed in a clean and snug little room instead

214

of in a prison cell I could not quite grasp, but I knew that there was not much point in continuing to live.

So, when the tray of well-prepared food, light and easily digested as befitted a supper for someone in delicate health, was set before me, I shook my head and closed my eyes.

'I don't want any,' I said.

'But you must eat,' insisted Mrs Hanley, and took a little broth in a spoon and held it to my lips.

'No,' I said, tears rolling down my cheeks. 'Leave me alone, and let me die.'

Vaguely, I had heard footsteps upon the stairs, and outside the door, but now that familiar and well-hated voice broke across poor Mrs Hanley's protests.

'They told me downstairs that she was better,' he said, stepping into my range of sight, neat and properly shaven and whip slim in his riding clothes.

'She won't eat,' announced Grace Hanley, helplessly.

'Oh?' Mr Lambert took the spoon into his own hand, brushing her aside, gently. 'We'll see about that. Now, Miss Furlong, behave yourself.'

I shook my head again.

'You're going to eat, even if I have to prop your jaws open with corks,' he threatened, and knowing Mr Lambert's determination, I yielded and swallowed the broth.

'You can leave us, Grace. I'll see to it that she finishes her supper.'

Mrs Hanley hesitated, plainly not liking the idea of leaving her cousin alone with me, but then she went, however seeing to it that the door was wide open.

'Now, what's all this rubbish about letting you die? You can't think we've nursed you day and night for that, Miss Furlong?'

'What's the use? I'm bound for the gallows,' I responded, dolefully, as soon as my mouth was empty.

'You're still delirious. No one is sending you to the gallows. Have some baked custard. Very strengthening.' Mr Lambert's face, as he plunged a spoon into the dish, did not show much personal enthusiasm for baked custard, but he pushed some into my mouth.

'You know that I killed a man at Port Albert,' I said, when I had swallowed it. 'Or have you schemed your way out of *that*?'

'You're a silly girl,' he chuckled, feeding me the rest of the custard. 'You only knocked him out cold. You don't know your own strength, Miss Furlong, and just as well. Thank you. You saved me from a serious injury.'

Then he sobered.

'You've been extremely ill. A chill, which developed into congestion of the lungs, complicated by brain fever. Fortunately, when the steamer arrived from Melbourne, the captain's wife was on board, and she helped nurse you on the voyage here. My cousin's husband is a physician, and they've been good enough to keep you here in their house.' He arose from the chair upon which he had been sitting, and in the lamplight his hair was burnished, almost coppery. 'I cannot thank God enough that He chose to spare you. When you're stronger, Miss Furlong, we have a lot to discuss.'

'Why do you call me Furlong?' Now that my mind was clearer, I remembered that Mr Lambert had never known me by any name but Smith, and that I had been Starling for a considerable time before that.

He paused on his way to the door.

'You rambled on endlessly while you were delirious,' he explained. Then, unexpectedly, he turned back, and bending over, kissed me lightly on the forehead. 'Thank you, for recovering, Miss Furlong. I'd wanted revenge and justice, but if you'd died, it would have weighed heavy on my conscience for the rest of my days.' He straightened up, while I regarded him with a mixture of emotions.

'I'll send the maid up for the tray.'

When he had gone, I lay back on my pillows, and turned things over in my mind. The first of these, and one which, being a normal young woman, I dwelled upon at length, was the fact of Mr Lambert kissing me. My first reaction had been to class him with such persons as my odious cousin Franklin, forever attempting to take advantage of young females, but almost immediately, I had to admit that this was unfair. Isaac Purtle had referred to Mr Lambert as a gentleman, and although I could not agree with this entirely, in one way it was true. Oh yes, Mr Lambert had slapped my face to prevent me falling into a fit of the vapours, and there had been times when his behaviour had been unkind, but upon no occasion had he taken advantage of our position.

After some minutes of mulling, I had to admit that I had not minded very much when Mr Lambert had kissed me. There had been nothing objectionable about it. It had been friendly, brotherly rather than lover-like, and yet, it did open up a train of thought. I was engaged to a man whom I still wished to marry, in spite of all the ugly complications, and I hoped that Mr Lambert would not make a habit of it.

Having disposed of this trivial, but highly important, occurrence, I wondered exactly what Mr Lambert had told his cousin and her husband, obviously respectable people, about me. Mrs Hanley, surely, could not be bluffed into thinking that I was Elizabeth Lambert. They knew me as Clytie Furlong, which made me wonder, anxiously, whether the law had reached as far as Port Phillip in its search for me. I could understand Mr Lambert using this knowledge to keep me under his thumb. Thinking of the law brought me back to those last moments at Port Albert, when Quentin Lambert had looked me straight in the face and denied being a criminal. And not a quarter of an hour since he had confessed to wanting 'revenge and justice.' I was not yet well enough to grapple with these questions, and I soon dozed off into another deep slumber.

Recovery was a slow affair, and how can I express my everlasting gratitude for the sheer kindness shown to me by Grace and Dr Hanley? I did not see very much of Mr Lambert. He was staying at a hotel, and had business, so Mrs Hanley told me, to keep him occupied here in Melbourne. He dropped in once each day, to exchange no more than a few words with me, and to make sure that I was recovering my health.

A dressmaker was sent to the house under his auspices, and I was measured up for new clothes and consulted about dress stuffs, although for my first days out of bed I made do with borrowed clothing. Not once did he mention our original arrangement until the day when he called and found me, for the first time, sitting in the back garden, and reading aloud from a book to little Jenny Hanley.

'Run along, moppet,' he said, kindly, to the little girl, and then he smiled at me. 'She reminds me of my young Bess, you know. Bess is a Lambert through and through, but Dolly is the image of her dear mother. I do miss them,' he added, sitting at my side and crossing his legs.

Mr Lambert had never before discussed his children with me, and I had learnt their names through course of conversation with Mrs Hanley, who had also informed me that his only son had died a week after birth, leaving Mrs Lambert in a state of poor health.

'When are you going back to Sydney?' I asked, wanting to know where I stood. Nothing further had been said about my part as the lost woman of Gipps Land, and I was wondering whether Mr Lambert had given up his plan.

'Soon, I hope. I can't afford to wait much longer.'

Wait? For what? I thought of my dyed hair beneath the muslin cap I wore, and determined to press the question, but he spoke again before I could find words.

'And now, Clytie Furlong, we are going to have our talk. You're the daughter of one William Furlong, and granddaughter of Frederick Furlong, and sister of Horace and Thomas Furlong.'

'Half-sister,' I corrected him, feeling my heart sink down to my feet.

'All right, half-sister. Now, Miss Furlong, why did you bolt from the Reeds' house when you heard that your family were looking for you? Because you thought they'd put a stop to you marrying a transported man?'

'If you know that much, you must know the rest.' My voice came out, low and strained. 'I — they thought I'd killed my grandfather.'

'That's odd.' Mr Lambert had looked startled, but only briefly. 'After Dr Hanley had shown me the advertisement in the *Port Phillip Herald* asking for information leading to the whereabouts of one Clytie Amanda Furlong, also known as Starling, I went to the lawyer handling it here. Your frantic relatives have been posting advertisements and offers of a reward in all the Australian colonies. I wonder,' he ruminated, 'whether I should apply for the reward myself?'

Then, funning over, he turned to me, grave and a little disturbed.

'You'd better tell me the whole story,' he commanded, and I did, from the first day I had arrived at Furlong Hall, a frightened, lonely girl, uncertain of my reception, and very conscious of my position in life. I told him of my grandfather's fall, of Mrs Furlong's drunken accusations, and my terror, which had culminated in my flight.

'But Clytie,' he said, puzzled, and using my given name for the first time, 'you were in a house full of servants, not to mention a few assorted relatives. They surely would have known that Mrs Furlong was a drunkard and that she wasn't to be taken seriously. It's more than that, isn't it? It has to do with those nightmares of yours, something about a woman called Antoinette.'

'I don't want to talk about it.'

'Come on, now. Get it all out.' He took my hand, which was trembling.

So I told him about the fortune teller's prophecy and how it had come true, and my grandfather's accident and Mrs Furlong's accusations. There was an expression of cynical disbelief on my listener's features, but he asked me about Antoinette.

'I hated her so much. She was my father's mistress, you see, and she'd persuaded him to send me back to England. I used to pray that she'd die, and she did, only my father was murdered too. If I hadn't wished such a dreadful thing, my poor father wouldn't . . . '

Mr Lambert let go my hand and took out a cigar, which he lit and puffed on before uttering another word, while I sat there quietly, making a rather strange discovery. I had never spoken of my guilt to another living soul, and now that I had, it all sounded extremely silly.

'A long time ago,' he murmured, 'a very wise man wrote that when he was a child, he spoke as a child, understood as a child, and thought as a child, but when he became a man, he put away childish things. Now, think about it, Clytie. How old were you when your father was murdered. Sixteen? A child still. If a person died every time someone else wished it, the human race would have become extinct centuries ago. As for the fortune teller — look over there!'

I looked in the direction of his nod. Annie, the Hanley's maid-of-all-work, had just come outside to empty a bucket of water.

'I'll tell you Annie's fortune. She's going to

hear of a birth, of a death, of an accident, an illness, and of someone's good luck. Death's a part of life, Clytie. Your father's death was so shocking that you've never recovered from the experience. As for fortune tellers — they're clever enough to know we all share the human experience, and that part of what they foretell must come true. As for what doesn't — we forget it. Now, put all that nonsense out of your head for good, and start thinking about your return to England.'

As I sat there, very quietly, I could hear about me all the ordinary sounds of every day living, a hen cackling in triumph as she laid an egg, horses in the street, children calling out, and nails being hammered into wood. Go back to England? To the doubtful and grudging charity of my father's family? I wanted to laugh out aloud. There was absolutely no reason now why I should not go straight to James Harkness. I was free, untrammelled, and my own mistress.

'Why? I am going to be married, Mr Lambert, here, to the man of my own choice. I think our bargain is complete, isn't it? I've done what you wanted, and nearly lost my life in the doing. But now, you see, I'm not frightened any more.'

I made to stand up, to walk away, to demonstrate my new liberty, but he had me by the wrist, in a grip so hard that I winced.

'You're going back to England! I won't let you throw away your life. Listen to me, Clytie.'

'Miss Furlong!' I corrected him, haughtily.

'Stop acting like a child. Now, listen. Your father's family are rich and powerful, and they've provided capital for some very big runs here in New South Wales. They want transportation resumed. You're pretty and intelligent, and you could influence them, even if you are from the wrong side of the Furlong blanket. They're thinking of easy profits, not of the future, Clytie. We want decent, honest people in this country. We want respectable young women who'll provide homes for men so that they'll have more to their lives than the grog shanties. Transportation is brutal, Clytie. It turns the victims into brutes, and their masters too.'

To my amazement, he let go of my wrist, jumped to his feet, flung off his coat, then his waistcoat, and jerked up his shirt at the back.

'Look,' he said, grimly. 'Look at it!'

I saw his back. From waist to shoulder, it was one mass of scar tissue, in a grotesque design of purple crisscross. Before I had finished uttering the ejaculation which came from my lips, he had pulled down his shirt, and was picking up his other garments and slipping them on.

'It was my bad luck,' he said, crisply, 'to be assigned to a fine gentleman called Mudie. Mr Mudie thought that I had ideas above my station because I complained about our rations and the hours we were forced to work. So I was tied to Mr Mudie's flogging tree and given a hundred of the best. I'm proud to say that I walked away afterwards, even though my boots overflowed with my own blood.'

He must have seen the incredulity on my face, because there was an addendum, delivered with a quiet, intense bitterness.

'I collapsed the instant I was out of that swine's sight.'

So I sat there, pulled three ways, between Jem, the family who seemed to want me after all, and the beginnings of a strange new sense, that I had a destiny for which my odd education and toughening experiences had prepared me. Mr Lambert, having adjusted his coat, found the remains of his cigar which he had placed carefully on the end of the garden seat, and began to walk away from me, just as Mrs Hanley came out of doors. She still wore her bonnet, plainly having just returned from her round of marketing, a chore which was usually the lot of the colonial housewife, for few servants were sufficiently well trained to undertake the responsibility.

'Quentin,' she cried. 'She's here. In Melbourne. I saw her. Not ten minutes since.'

17

No hint was given as to whom 'she' might be, and Mr Lambert immediately took his cousin by the arm and hurried her inside. I followed, chewing thoughtfully on my lower lip. Something I had learnt in this house was that Mrs Hanley was considerably under her strong-minded cousin's thumb, and I realised, by the elation on Mr Lambert's face and the speed with which he whisked her out of earshot, that 'she' was extremely important to him.

Now, could it be that his anxiety to prove that Mrs Lambert was truly dead could have been for the most elementary and obvious reason of all? That he wished to marry again? No, that did not make sense, did not fit in with the dying of my hair and his talk of revenge and justice. I was all a-prickle with curiosity, and had learnt a thing or two about eavesdropping during my childhood, when prior knowledge of the relations between my father and his current mistress had a decided bearing upon my wellbeing. So, I went inside without attempting to be quiet, and walked upstairs in a normal manner. Immediately, I crept down again, and leaned over the rail about halfway down, so that I could better hear Mr Lambert and his cousin.

'But the poor girl has been so ill,' said Grace, reprovingly. 'Oh, Quentin, you could have been wrong all along. And if you are right, you could be putting Miss Furlong to fearful risk.'

'I have the bait,' said Mr Lambert, implacably. 'I won't allow any harm to come to Miss Furlong. Believe that, Grace. I'm going to see that she's safely delivered back to her family in England. I owe her that. Now, Grace, LeFevre's back from Gipps Land. It's all over town. There was a great falling out in his party, but he's got wind that I brought a woman back to Port Albert.' I could imagine Mr Lambert rubbing his hands in glee, and the devils dancing in his eyes. 'It couldn't be better, Grace. Couldn't be better. Our lady friend 'll lose her fortune yet.'

So, here it was again. Villainy! Our fox had been masquerading very nicely over the past days, acting out the part of kindly and concerned mentor of my well-being, arousing my sympathy by showing me his scars, and almost convincing me with all his lofty talk of my using my influence with my family for the betterment of mankind.

Hastily, I slipped up to my room, and

closed the door. What could I do now? My first impulse was to pack what little I now possessed, and set out to find Jem, but as I sank on to the chair, my knees felt so weak that I was reminded that I had not yet fully recovered my strength. My mind returned to what I had planned in Port Albert, and lingered there. Fate had intervened to stop me then, but perhaps only so that I should have a much better opportunity later. I had to move cautiously, obtain all the evidence possible, and above all, *find out what it was all about.*

Mr LeFevre pounced that very evening, whilst Mr Lambert, Grace Hanley and myself were at dinner. Dr Hanley was absent, having been called away urgently to attend to the injuries of a young squatter who had fallen from his horse whilst celebrating his stay in town rather too riotously. Mr Lambert talked about trivialities, Mrs Hanley appeared abstracted and kept sending me strange looks, and I chattered on as if nothing were amiss. Then the maid announced the arrival of a visitor, and Grace went out, to return in half a minute, frowning uneasily.

'Quentin,' she said, almost accusingly, 'Mr LeFevre's here, in the drawing room, and he's demanding to see Miss Furlong.'

Mr Lambert dabbed at his lips with his

napkin before arising.

'And so he shall,' he said mildly. 'We'll face him together. Come along, Clytie.'

So, I thought crossly, I'm Clytie in front of Mrs Hanley now. Mr Lambert must have taken my annoyance for trepidation, because he gently squeezed my arm, and said, 'Don't worry' softly in my ear.

Mr LeFevre, dressed to the nines as if he were on the way to a grand reception, bowed to me stiffly.

'A thousand pardons for interrupting your dinner,' he said, with a most notable absence of that foul language which had characterised his every utterance when we had met before, 'but I've heard rumours. Most disturbing rumours. Ahem.'

I think that he was taken aback at my appearance, for I was nicely dressed in a new dress, with a light shawl draped about my shoulders in deference to the coolness of the October evening, and my hair was covered prettily with a dainty cap, unusual perhaps in a young unmarried woman, but quite becoming.

'Rumours?' asked Mr Lambert, heavily, as if preparing to defend my honour.

'Yes. Ahem. We met once before, Lambert.'

'So I recollect. A sad occasion. How can I help you now?'

'I've had it on good authority that when you returned to Port Albert you had in your company a young woman. I've also learnt that when you arrived in Melbourne, a young woman was brought ashore, extremely ill, and transported here to this house.'

'Yes, you heard correctly.'

'I demand to know under what circumstances you met this young woman, Mr Lambert. There's been a great deal of public money spent — I hesitate to say wasted — upon expeditions into Gipps Land seeking a woman supposed to be held prisoner by the blacks.'

'I fail to see what this has to do with Miss Furlong.' Mr Lambert was very much upon his dignity, and in spite of the seriousness of the matter, I had difficulty in repressing a giggle.

Mr LeFevre's protuberant eyes flashed from one to the other of us before he spoke again, heavily.

'I think Lambert, that you're prevaricating.'

Mr Lambert's shoulders shrugged.

'Think what you like. All I ask is that you remember that you're a gentleman, and say nothing to injure Miss Furlong's reputation. I admit that it fell to me to escort her from Gipps Land under — er — somewhat unusual circumstances. Beyond that, I've nothing to say.'

Mr LeFevre swung about to face me.

'Well?' he barked. 'What've *you* to say, Miss Furlong?'

Mr Lambert immediately placed himself between us.

'Miss Furlong has been extremely ill. I suggest, LeFevre, that you stop tormenting her with your baseless accusations and leave this house.'

Mr LeFevre looked fit to explode, and yet there was something else besides anger in his eyes. There was that look of puzzlement which comes to people when they think they recognise someone but are not quite sure. It was my opportunity to blurt out the truth, but two things made me hold my tongue. One was that I was now determined to discover exactly what Mr Lambert conspired and hand him over to justice with all the evidence tied neatly in a bundle. The other was that I had disliked Mr LeFevre from the first moment of seeing him.

Our visitor made a gobbling noise, reminiscent of that uttered by the inquisitive emu which had awakened me one fine morning in Gipps Land. Then he picked up his hat.

'It's obvious to me that you're both hiding the truth from the public. I intend to carry this to a higher authority.'

When he had gone, Mr Lambert grinned, as if savouring a very tasty morsel.

'It'll be all over town by morning,' he said, 'that the Miss Furlong staying with the Hanley's is the white woman of Gipps Land.'

'Oh,' I returned. 'I'm to be made into a circus freak? The woman who lived like a lubra? Mr Lambert, I am engaged to be married. How do you think my future husband will feel?'

'Does it matter so much?'

His cold-blooded audacity left me speechless, and he began talking again, quickly.

'I've been waiting for the right moment to tell you. I tracked down your fiancé and, well, he's already married. Two months ago, and the baby's due in four. The girl's parents are respectable folk, and they kicked up a fuss.'

'You're lying.'

'I'm not. I thought if I could persuade you to decide that going back to England was better than settling in the bush, it wouldn't matter too much. Clytie, did you really want to marry a young man who's been transported for beating an old woman nearly to death for six shillings and two pence?'

I put my hands over my ears.

'Stop it! You're a liar. Everything you say

is a lie. I've never detested anyone — I didn't know I could despise anyone — as much as I hate and loathe you.'

'Detest, despise, hate and loathe! Congratulations, Miss Furlong. You've covered the whole field of dislike. Now come along and let's finish our dinner.'

If this had been my own house, I would have bolted upstairs and slammed my door, but just in time, self-respect held me back from such a display of dramatics. I had to save all those scalding tears for later, when they drenched my pillow and gave some ease to my wounded pride. What Quentin Lambert had said about Jem was the truth. I had to admit it. Mrs Reed had warned me against the handsome overseer when I was at the height of my passion for him, and I had disregarded her advice. James Harkness had not really wanted to marry me. He had made an empty promise because he had hoped that once he had left the Reeds' home property, he would be out of my reach.

The next morning, I sat with Grace Hanley in a narrow little room at the side of the house, an afterthought which provided a place for sewing, letter writing, or shelter for the children in wet weather.

It already seems strange that so short a time ago, women were slaves to the needle. What freedom Mr Singer's invention has brought to womankind, and his little machine must be accounted one of the major benefits of the industrial age. Mrs Hanley was not poor, but this was a pioneer town in the early forties, and female servants were scarce. Thus, the lady of the house had to perform many tasks which elsewhere would be left to menials, and as a guest, it was only polite that I should also take up needle and thread as Grace brought out the curtains she was hemming.

We stitched in silence for a while. I was full of my own thoughts, and it could not have been lost on her that when her cousin and myself had returned to the dinner table the previous evening, we were not on speaking terms.

'You really are like poor Elizabeth,' she said, snipping a thread with her little silver scissors.

'I believe so. That is why Mr Lambert chose me for whatever it is he had in mind.'

'I don't mean your looks. The resemblance is only passing. I mean that you don't allow Quentin to browbeat you. Neither did Elizabeth.'

This caused me some surprise, for I had long since classified poor Mrs Lambert, on the flimsiest of evidence, as a doormat.

'Quentin likes his own way. We're cousins twice over, you know, and I think that is why we are so close. Our fathers were brothers, and our mothers sisters. My parents died while I was young, and I was brought up in Uncle Richard's home.'

'Really?' I said, politely, setting my stitches with exaggerated care.

'Miss Furlong, Clytie, oh, I don't know what to tell you. But do believe me. Quentin is a good man. There is a debt he wishes to settle.'

'Which is why he'd do anything for money, no doubt.'

Grace Hanley put down her sewing, and stared at me, her face a softer, sweet version of Mr Lambert's, right down to a tendency to freckle.

'Clytie, Quentin has no need of money. He's a very wealthy man. It's a debt of another kind. I know he has used you, and not very kindly, but if only you understood! He should have told you the whole story, but when you first met, he thought you were just a common little guttersnipe, an adventuress living by your wits.'

I gritted my teeth at this last, but said nothing, eager to hear Grace's story.

'My uncle is a poor country clergyman,

the best and most generous man imaginable. The boys were well educated, but there was no money, and they had to find their own way in life. Now Quentin had a good post as a tutor in a wealthy household, but while he was visiting his parents, he heard that soldiers had been sent into our county because of trouble amongst the farm workers. This was just before the Reform Bill, and times were very difficult. There was a lot of rick burning and the like in our district, and Quentin knew that some of the lads he had played with as a child were involved. He met them, to try to talk them out of what they were doing, but he was too late. He was arrested, along with nine others, and accused of treason. Seven of those poor, foolish lads, Miss Furlong, were hanged. Three, including Quentin, were transported. Quentin spoke up at his trial, saying that it was injustice, not disloyalty, which had made those young men act as they did, and for his pains his sentence was extended to the term of his natural life.

'Well, after some very bad times, he came to the notice of Mr Eldridge, Elizabeth's father. Mr Eldridge worked very hard on Quentin's behalf but, in the end, when Quentin received his pardon, it was on condition that he remained in New South

Wales. He was bitterly disappointed. My uncle has been an invalid for many years, and unable to travel as far as New South Wales, and Quentin dearly longs to see him again, I think to show him that in spite of everything, he has made a success of his life. Still, Mr Eldridge had taken him into his business, and Quentin married Elizabeth. Mr Eldridge then retired to his property in Van Diemen's Land but, sad to say, when Mr Eldridge married again, there was a falling-out.'

Grace picked up her sewing again. She appeared to be turning something over in her mind, perhaps wondering if she should tell me the rest. As for my part, I was thinking of the well-bred young man sent to languish amidst the crude, foul-mouthed ruffians who made up the bulk of the convict population in New South Wales. Then, before either of us could utter a word, Annie, the maid, came in to tell her mistress that there was a caller, a Mrs Eldridge, who was insisting upon seeing Mrs Lambert.

18

Poor Annie was absolutely confused, as well she might have been, but now Grace Hanley, who had been so irresolute only seconds before, was all decision.

'Annie, run quickly across the road to the Arms, and tell Mr Lambert that Mrs Eldridge is here. Go out of the back door. Now, hurry!' Then she turned to me, and laid a plump hand upon my arm. 'I'll talk to her first. Don't worry. Everything'll be all right.'

She bustled out of the room, leaving me almost as flustered as Annie, who had already dashed off on her errand. As had happened a hundred times since I had met Mr Lambert, nothing made sense. Even Mrs Hanley had admitted that I did not closely resemble Elizabeth Lambert. I could not believe that the plotters would permit me to be seen by Mrs Eldridge, who would instantly recognise me as an imposter, and now I was sure that the reason for Mr Lambert's excitement (alarm?) on hearing that his wife's stepmother had arrived in Melbourne was fear of exposure. I resolved to see Mrs Eldridge at all costs, and tell her everything. Now that I knew that my fears of being arrested and extradited to Britain were groundless, I had no intention of finding myself in prison. I liked Grace Hanley, was grateful to her for her kindness, and I appreciated that her fondness for her cousin had prompted her attempt to present him to me in a better light. But now that I had a new future, I was not going to throw it away. I was sick of being misused by men, whether they be heartless flirts or scheming criminals. Something inside of me — that weak little part which had enjoyed being kissed by Mr Lambert and was moved to sympathy by the story of a young man too proud to reveal the agonies of his pulped flesh — stirred, and I crushed it mercilessly. Experience had taught me that everyone in this world used someone else, and that this was the way to survive.

I could hear the two women talking, Grace soft and uncertain, the other arrogant and just a little common in voice.

'Mrs Hanley, I *know* that Elizabeth is here. The whole town's talking about the woman Quentin brought back from Gipps Land. I demand to see her.'

I waited no longer, but walked out purposefully towards the drawing room, almost to collide with Grace.

'Go in,' she whispered, 'she's waiting for you. Don't worry. Everything will be all right.'

This made nonsense of my earlier supposition, that Mr Lambert and Mrs Hanley would wish to keep me from the visitor's sight.

The drawing room, was actually more of a parlour, for this house was too small to boast of much pretension, and Mrs Eldridge's wide skirts seemed to take up most of the vacant space between the furniture. She was tall, slim, very well-dressed, with silk ruching under the brim of her bonnet to frame a handsome, haughty face. For a moment, I was shocked, for she was so like Antoinette, and yet when I gathered my senses, I could see that there was little similarity in their features. What they had in common was an aura, a something, a hardness, perhaps, which comes to women who take what they want from life. To give Antoinette her due, she had lived only for fresh sensations in love. This Mrs Eldridge had the sleeker air of one who craves money and knows how to find it.

She stared at me, blankly, as if unable to believe her eyes.

'But you're not Elizabeth!' she exclaimed. 'What rubbish is this!'

She reached forward, quickly, and before I could duck out of the way, had snatched away the muslin cap I wore over my dyed and ragged locks, to glare, hard-mouthed, at the tell-tale fair roots.

I was at a loss for words. At this moment of dénouement, the whole thing seemed so silly, so futile, and so unlikely an enterprise for a man of Quentin Lambert's undoubted intelligence. Mrs Eldridge was the first to speak.

'Quentin!' she exclaimed, and I turned to see him, pokerfaced, in the doorway.

'I thought you'd come when you heard the rumours,' he said, very quietly.

'Of course. When I heard that you'd brought a woman resembling Elizabeth out of the bush to Port Albert, and on to Melbourne, what should I do but take ship here to see if a miracle had happened?'

'And, no doubt, you brought your inheritance powder with you?'

Mrs Eldridge's handsome face became just a shade harder, and yet, at the same time, a certain flicker passed through her eyes, to be replaced almost instantly by a stony stare.

'What rubbish is this? You don't change, do you Quentin? Always making mischief. And what do you hope to gain by foisting this — this girl on to the public as the lost white woman?'

'What is inheritance powder?' I interpolated. After all, I was an important player in this drama.

'Arsenic,' said Mr Lambert, still in that hushed, yet threatening, voice.

Now I saw that Mrs Eldridge had left her reticule upon a small lacquered table, and although she laughed outright at Mr Lambert, she edged one hand towards this accessory. I was quicker, and grabbed it, and handed it to Mr Lambert, why I do not really know to this day, except that I wanted the whole complicated affair finished and over.

'Give me that, you little slut!' Mrs Eldridge fairly jumped towards me, but Mr Lambert was already undoing the string, and he withdrew a small stoppered bottle containing white powder.

'I use it for my complexion,' snapped Mrs Eldridge.

There was another man standing behind Mr Lambert now, a stranger to me, and Mr Lambert gave him the bottle.

'This man is a magistrate, Cora. You won't object if he arranges to have the contents analysed?'

'Why should I? You can see how white my skin is. I use arsenic as a cosmetic.'

She laughed. 'Good heavens, Quentin! What you'll do for money! Are you hoping to make me a murderess so that you can put your hands on my poor dear husband's fortune?'

Now, I dithered again. This is what I had thought all along, that Mr Lambert was after money, but now his voice, calm, and with no laughter to match hers, cut across the beginning of her next sentence.

'My wife was desperately sick after she left Launceston to return to Sydney, and that is what saved her from the shipwreck. One of the seamen, a Maori, and an old friend of mine, is an exceptionally powerful swimmer like many of his race, and when the ship ran into trouble, he made it his business to save Elizabeth. Her symptoms suggested cholera, but Maori Mick told me something which made me suspicious. Even as the ship foundered, she clung to a small bottle of white powder, which she said was medicine to help her poor state of health.'

'What rubbish!' Mrs Eldridge turned to the magistrate. 'Surely you can't believe this pack of lies! More likely he gave his wife the medicine himself. After all, who is this slut?'

'Don't call Miss Furlong a slut, Cora. She's the bait. The bait which brought you here. I think I have enough proof, with this pretty little bottle, to see about having my father-in-law's remains exhumed and examined.'

'And what will that prove?' Mrs Eldridge was openly scoffing. 'A cock and bull story handed on by a savage, a *fal-de-lal* about this trollop — your mistress — pretending to be your wife!'

'Miss Furlong is not a trollop. She is not my mistress, and she has never pretended to be my wife. Neither have I at any time suggested that I brought my wife from Gipps Land, where she lies buried, God rest her dear soul. And, Cora, I have her last letter, despatched on another ship a few days before she sailed herself. She believed her father's illness to be due to a form of chronic dysentery, but she also mentioned your kindness in giving her a remedy for the female troubles which had distressed her since our poor little son was born. That, coupled with the fact that Mr Eldridge altered his will — influenced by your dislike of me — *before* my wife's death, should be enough.'

'And if you can have my dear husband's remains exhumed, what will that prove?' She still appeared confident.

'Probably that his body is full of arsenic.'

Her laugh rang out full and true.

'Rubbish!' she declared. It seemed to be her favourite expression, and she said it in such a determined way that few would have disbelieved her.

'You haven't heard of Marie LaFarge. Of course, Cora, you've never been much of a one for reading, have you? Marie was a Frenchwoman who decided to kill her husband, about four years ago. To her great misfortune, science had just discovered a way to prove that her husband's remains contained arsenic. She is now in prison, and will be there for the rest of her life. British juries aren't as easily swayed by a pretty face, Cora.'

This time, she did show some reaction. Her eyes dilated, and although she said 'Rubbish!' it was entirely without conviction.

Later, I was given some details to fill in my part in this extraordinary story. Mr Lambert's original intention had been to find the body of his wife, in the somewhat remote hope that the bottle of arsenic powder was still in her pocket. News of a white woman being held captive by the blacks, and my sudden arrival in his life, had combined to give him the inspiration of trying to make Cora Eldridge act with sufficient rashness to enable him to request that his father-in-law's body should be exhumed.

Much later, I heard that Cora Eldridge was brought to trial, and after long-drawn-out proceedings, was sentenced to life imprisonment. Like Marie LaFarge, she soon succumbed to consumption, and few mourned her passing. The estate went to Mr Lambert's children and other relatives of Mr Eldridge's who still lived in Britain.

My job as 'bait' was over, and with Mr LeFevre rushing from one official to another demanding an enquiry into Mr Lambert's activities, my tormentor, or master, or benefactor, depending upon my mood of the moment, resorted to the guile which had gained him his nickname.

He had ascertained that there was a suitable ship standing off the mouth of Melbourne's River Yarra Yarra, and before the week was out, I was on my way back to Britain.

★ ★ ★

Early one morning, I was driven to the nearby river wharf, there to embark, with Mr Lambert, on a small steamer which took out into Port Phillip Bay, and my ship. This was my first, and only, excursion through the streets of Melbourne. It was not very impressive, another pioneer town, with holes in the roadway and cows wandering about, and houses surrounded by vegetable patches. Some aboriginals were camped at an intersection, and a wretchedly grubby lot they were, the drunken remnants of the tribe which had sold its birthright for a few axes and blankets to the town's founder, John Batman, already dead in his thirties from his excessive dissipations. I thought of the proud, crafty Bungelene and his saucy young lubra, and wanted to weep.

On board ship, Mr Lambert inspected my cabin with all his usual briskness. He did not linger, for we were due to sail almost immediately, and in any case, he was in a hurry to go aboard the other vessel which would take him back to Sydney.

'Well, Clytie,' he said, as we stood on deck in bright sunshine, 'this is goodbye. It's unlikely you'll ever come back to New South Wales, and I can't leave.'

At least, I thought, he's calling me Clytie again. I had been Miss Furlong ever since the night of Mr LeFevre's visit. How strange it was, that although there had been at least a dozen occasions upon which I had wished Mr Lambert in Hades, I now dreaded leaving him.

'You don't feel too badly about that young man?'

I shook my head. Grace had told me how I

249

had called out for Jem, and how Mr Lambert had ridden off in search of him, only to discover that not only had James Harkness married, but he had virtually forgotten me. Mrs Hanley and her cousin had mutually decided to keep it from me until I had recovered my health. I was hurt, but knew that I had had an escape.

'I'm glad. There'll be another young man, someone better, and more your equal. You've talent and intelligence. Don't waste them. You weren't meant to spend the rest of your life in a bush shack.'

It was time for him to go, and having said his piece about my future, he held out his hand in farewell.

'I — you know I didn't mean it when I said that I hated you. I'm ashamed that I was so rude.'

He grinned, slowly, in response to my halting words.

'I knew that at the time, Clytie. You were badly treated, and I don't blame you for being so upset. Write to me when you arrive. Here's my card, and if things don't go well with the Furlongs, my parent's address is on the back. Go to them. In any case, I hope you'll visit them.'

I glanced down at the card, at his father's name written in a neat hand.

'Rev Richard Fox-Lambert.'

My eyebrows must have shot up, because he laughed.

'I earned my nickname honestly, as you see. I dropped the Fox in the hope that I could lose it, but . . . Now, I must go. Goodbye, Clytie. In spite of all our little differences, I hope you'll try to remember me in a favourable light.'

He shook my hand, warmly, and I ran to the rail and watched as he was rowed to shore, and when he looked back, I waved furiously. Already, a growing sense of loss was descending upon me.

Don't be silly, I told myself, as the breeze filled our sails and the whole ship quivered into life. It's all over.

But, as I should have known by then, one does not leave the past so easily behind.

19

The voyage back to England was uneventful, with such things as whales seen in the distance (and what an anti-climax their famous blowing proved to be — not at all like those dramatic pictures dreamed up by artists safely on shore) and passing birds and bright sunsets providing hours of conversation to while away the tedium. The lady with whom I shared my cabin worked assiduously at her petit point, and daily made a great to-do about it.

'Look,' she would say, with the most enormous satisfaction, 'another leaf done and one square inch of background filled in,' and I envied the calm mind which could use so little to use so much time.

I kept a journal which, instead of an account of our daily doings and the state of the weather, turned into a collection of reminiscences about my life in New South Wales. We passengers were told that if we met with a ship on the way 'out,' there would be an exchange of mail, so I prepared by writing a letter of thanks to Grace Hanley, one of explanation and apology to Mrs Reed, and yet another to Mr Lambert. In this, I merely mentioned that my lingering cough had cleared up, and that my quarters were comfortable and one or two other common-places. We finally did have the good fortune to meet another ship, bound for Sydney, and at the last moment I enclosed two small sketches I had made of our shipboard life, just to show Mr Lambert that I was occupied and happy, and not moping in any way.

Eventually, I found myself once again in the company of my cousin Franklin Parker — and his wife, with whom he had affected a reconcilation. She was, and still is, a charming lady, and it was from her that I learnt what had happened after my sudden departure from Furlong Hall.

My grandfather had not died, as I knew now, and my timid spinster cousins came forward to say that they had seen what had occurred, and that Grandfather had fallen as a result of his stroke. As soon as he learnt that I had bolted, Cousin Franklin began a search, for a while without success. In the end, he placed notices in several newspapers, and included in my description that I usually wore a silver cross of Italian manufacture on a chain about my neck. Perhaps this gift from our servants back in Naples brought me the protection they had promised it would, for it led Franklin to Liverpool, where he finally ascertained that a Miss Clytie Starling had been sent to New South Wales on a 'bride' ship. He immediately despatched enquiries to the agents who handled the Furlongs' business in New South Wales, but the vessel carrying the letter foundered. Thus, over two years had elapsed before that Sunday when the magistrate arrived at the Reeds' home asking for me.

'And a fine dance you've led us,' grumbled Franklin, as we set out upon the railway for Furlong Hall. 'Ungrateful brat. Should've left you there, only I daresay your brothers 'd have kicked up a fuss if I hadn't done something. And the old man. You needn't worry about *her*, Clytie, *she* went from bad to worse. Sent her away under the care of a nurse. Sad business.'

I was older now, and better able to understand the destructive forces unleashed when my father's irresponsibility had met the Furlong ambition head on. He had left his wife bitter and so unhappy that she drank her way into insanity, he had taken my own mother off into disgrace, homesickness and an early death from a Neapolitan fever, and his own bright idealism had been frittered away.

Yet how could I hate my grandfather, the real author of all this calamity? He was confined now to a chair, a poor, frail old man, who, although he saw in me the physical reincarnation of his wife, was otherwise quite in possession of his mental faculties. He asked me endless questions about New South Wales, which I answered as sensibly and truthfully as I was able, at the same time keeping in mind what Quentin Lambert had said to me.

My wild jaunt into Gipps Land I kept to myself, knowing that it would not be received with favour, but I did my best to explain that transported men were not, in the long run, the most economical form of labour. They were unwilling, mostly of poor character, and frequently of low mentality. I did not press the moral side of the question, that transportation was slavery in a different guise, and unworthy of a country which had led the way in the suppression of the ghastly African trade. Both my grandfather, and Franklin, who was now the real manager of the Furlong enterprises, were not swayed by emotional arguments, but seeing their profit hurt by indifferent workers was something else again. Furlong support was withdrawn from the transportation lobby, which, with loud noises from the squatting class in Australia, was working powerfully in Westminster again.

Now, my position had to be settled. My half-brothers arranged that the income which had supported my father should come to me during my lifetime, and it was decided that I should live with Horace, now a London lawyer. This, of course, had to be done with careful regard for the respectable façade the Furlongs presented to the world. Mrs Birrell was brought in to manage his household, and I was designated his cousin and her companion. This was another of the times when I have wished that my father had given more thought to how complicated he had made life for others.

Amidst all the seriousness, there were pleasant surprises. I had been in England no longer than six weeks when there arrived an oiled silk package, containing most of the sketches I had executed during my time with the Reeds. Even better, there was a long covering letter. Mr Lambert had visited them, he wrote, and had smoothed things over, and had obtained from them my sketchbook. So, naturally, I wrote and thanked him, and before very long, had another letter answering the one I had written during my voyage home. So, in spite of the slow mails in those days, what with my letter I had written as soon as I arrived safely, and the letter of thanks for my sketchbook, and the reply to the one in answer to my shipboard note, our correspondence was quite brisk, although it remained always on a newsy, unsentimental plane.

Through these letters, I learnt of the trial and conviction of Mrs Eldridge, and sadly, of Bungelene's tragic fate. The story for the missing white woman died hard, and agitation, from official circles which had no practical knowledge of the wild conditions in Gipps Land, continued to prod and probe. Eventually, a whisper, passed on perhaps by a rival tribesman, reached Mr Tyers, the Gipps Land Lands Commissioner, that Bungelene of the Kurnai had a white woman amongst his wives. The poor wretch was taken prisoner, and when questioned, said that the white woman had died, and pending further investigations, he was held captive.

When he read of this in a newspaper, Mr Lambert had gone immediately to the Colonial Secretary's office, there to tell as much of our story as necessary for Bungelene's release, for, he wrote, it was perfectly plain that a wild rumour had originated from the chance of Bungelene's wives witnessing Elizabeth Lambert's death. He was too late. Bungelene, as wild and free in body and spirit as the great eagles we had seen soaring above the Gipps Land forests, had been unable to endure imprisonment, and had pined to death.

It made me sad, and thoughtful, too. There was always a lot of talk in New South Wales about the wretched lives led by black women, and this had partly prompted the hysteria over the fate of the supposedly captive white woman. I remembered Bungelene's saucy young lubra, and found myself wondering whether her lot was worse than that of our poorer class women, worn out by childbearing and too often drink sodden wrecks at thirty.

During those terrible days in the Hungry Forties, I had chance enough of observing my less fortunate countrywomen, for my brother Horace increasingly immersed himself in the work of alleviating the plight of the poor. Through this, I had the pleasure of meeting again Mrs Caroline Chisholm, who had returned to Britain. My brothers gave her Family Colonization Loan Society all the support they could, and through its auspices, the British Government was persuaded to allow free passage of the wives and children of men who had been earlier transported. Mrs Chisholm referred to wives and children as 'God's police', and there can be no doubt that they had a more settling effect upon lonely men than any amount of preaching or any number of religious tracts.

This mellowing attitude on the part of the authorities made me determine to do a little campaigning of my own.

'You should marry, Clytie,' said my brother, Tom, severely. 'You're turning into a regular old maid busybody.'

Perhaps he was right. My life these days did seem to consist largely of good works, whether I was helping in a Ragged School, selling some of my sketches to help pay for schoolroom supplies, or addressing a select meeting about the problems of emigration. Yet, too often, I felt restless and constricted. Sometimes, I lay awake of a night and thought back to my adventures in Gipps Land, which had gained a romantic gloss with the passing of time. I forgot the mosquitoes and Isaac Purtle's horrible cooking, and the times when I had been outright scared. Instead, I remembered the good things like our companionship, the fresh smell of the bushland, and Mr Lambert placing his rolled up coat beneath my head.

Tom grumbled as I explained. So many years had elapsed. The man seemed to have done very well for himself in the colonies, and in any case, what is he to you, young woman?

An acquaintance, I said, catching a glimpse of myself in the gleaming glass doors which protected Tom's books from London's smuts. I could not help wondering what Mr Lambert would think of me now, with my well-brushed fair hair arranged fashionably, and the deep shot silk of my afternoon dress emphasizing the blue of my eyes. Actually, to say that this fresh attempt to clear Mr Lambert's name was entirely my idea is false. He wrote often about his daughters, to whom he was devoted, and how he hated to think of them growing up with the stigma of convictism attached to their name.

'I often think,' said Tom, putting on his spectacles and taking up his pen, 'that things happened in New South Wales which you have preferred not to explain to us.'

I thought of Tom, so straitlaced and earnest, and so determined to make up for our father's wasted life with his own, learning about my jaunt into the wilderness with three very assorted men, and had to suppress a burst of unseemly mirth.

These new efforts were successful, and Mr Lambert's sentence was rescinded completely, so that it was as if he had never been arrested, tried and transported. It would not make up for those grim years when he had been a prisoner of the Crown, nor would it erase the physical scars from his body, but he would be free to leave New South Wales if he wished.

The news was despatched officially, and I wrote joyfully that I was glad that I had been able to play a small part in righting a great injustice. How strange it was, I scrawled, allowing my pen to run away in my happiness, that the foolish ragamuffin of a girl who was forever bolting from one predicament to another should have in the end been in a position to help him. It was as if destiny had thrown us together, for without his sound advice and guidance, I may never have been in a position to return the favour.

It was the most high-flown piece of nonsense I have penned in all my life, and to it I received no reply.

Even allowing for the most wayward of winds, it became obvious that Mr Lambert considered our correspondence at an end. I enquired at Lloyd's to ascertain whether any ships from Australia had been lost lately, and received a negative reply. I could have kicked myself. Quentin Lambert had used me again. His name was cleared, his daughters were freed of the convict stigma, and Clytie, natural but accepted daughter of the House of Furlong, had made a fool of herself.

While I was in this bitter and uncertain frame of mind, I received a proposal of marriage. He was a fine man, a clergyman (like Mr Ellett who had been so kind to me and who had been married for several years), and my brothers approved of him, especially Tom, who had never managed to overcome his often apparent feelings that I was an embarrassment. But my faith in myself and my judgement had crumbled, and I grew thin and nervous, and a prey to my old fancies. It seemed only too obvious that the easy way in which Mr Lambert had explained away the grim prophecy of the old fortune teller had been part of his scheme to use me to his own ends. When he had found out that I had such powerful connections, he must have been hardly able to credit his own luck!

Oh, he had earned that Foxy nickname! At least, the *lazzaroni* class of Naples had made no pretence to be other than that what they were, thieves and tricksters.

The temptation to find escape and security in marriage was strong, but I was afraid to commit myself. Twice now I had been in love — why deny it, why else had I written so often to Mr Lambert? — and twice I had been hurt. I began having my bad dreams again, and Mrs Birrell took things in hand.

'The girl needs a holiday. We'll go to Bath.

Oh, I know its old fashioned and dowdy these days, but I've old friends there, and the change'll do Clytie good. And she'll be able to come to a wise decision without you, Horace, and your brother trying to make up her mind for her!'

I stood on the doorstep watching the servants load our luggage into the carriage which was to take us to the railway station. It was a beautiful morning, a morning for lovers, with no hint of the smoky clouds which had hidden the sun for days, and with the trees in the square bursting into their first young green.

A few yards along the roadway, a cab came to a halt. Out of this vehicle, a man sprang briskly, almost before the horse had halted. I was down our steps in a trice, and had covered those few yards in less time than it takes to think about it.

'Well,' said Mr Lambert, drily, holding out a warning hand to stop me from flinging myself into his arms, 'I can see that you haven't changed much. You're still rushing into things.'

★ ★ ★

Later, I heard of that agonisingly slow voyage, of calms followed by fierce gales which blew the ship right off course, and the fears of all on board that they would never reach their destination.

'I thought you'd forgotten me,' I said, still hardly able to credit that he was here, sitting at my side, and holding my hand as if he would never let it go. The trip to Bath, of course, had been instantly cancelled.

'Forgotten you? No, I hadn't forgotten you, but — what I hadn't expected is how pretty you are.' He seemed suddenly diffident. 'I'm too old for you, Clytie.'

I took a very deep breath.

'Quentin,' I announced, 'is that why you've come thirteen thousand miles — to tell me that you're too old for me?'

'I came thirteen thousand miles because it seemed quicker than writing to you and telling you to come to me! Oh, my dearest girl, all those stiff little schoolgirl letters, as if you were writing to an uncle because you had to! And you seemed so happy and well settled here, I didn't think . . . But that last letter made me realise that my hopes weren't in vain. Dammit girl, let's stop all this talk, and get married!'

We did, as soon as was decently possible, and as he has often remarked, we have argued happily ever since.

We do hope that you have enjoyed reading this large print book.

Did you know that all of our titles are available for purchase?

We publish a wide range of high quality large print books including:
Romances, Mysteries, Classics, General Fiction, Non Fiction and Westerns.

Special interest titles available in large print are:
The Little Oxford Dictionary
Music Book
Song Book
Hymn Book
Service Book

Also available from us courtesy of Oxford University Press:
Young Readers' Dictionary
(large print edition)
Young Readers' Thesaurus
(large print edition)

For further information or a free brochure, please contact us at:
Ulverscroft Large Print Books Ltd.,
The Green, Bradgate Road, Anstey,
Leicester, LE7 7FU, England.
Tel: (00 44) 0116 236 4325
Fax: (00 44) 0116 234 0205

THE WORLD AT NIGHT

Alan Furst

Jean Casson, a well-dressed, well-bred Parisian film producer, spends his days in the finest cafes and bistros, his evenings at elegant dinner parties and nights in the apartments of numerous women friends — until his agreeable lifestyle is changed for ever by the German invasion. As he struggles to put his world back together and to come to terms with the uncomfortable realities of life under German occupation, he becomes caught up — reluctantly — in the early activities of what was to become the French Resistance, and is faced with the first of many impossible choices.